ALL I SEE IS YOU

CHARLOTTE BARNES

Print ISBN 978-1-913942-48-9

ALSO BY CHARLOTTE BARNES

PSYCHOLOGICAL THRILLER

Intention

CRIME THRILLERS

The Copycat

The Watcher

The Cutter

PART I

ME

It seems strange to confess to something that you don't know for certain you've done.

At heart, I'm an honest person. One of my earliest memories is of finding a man's wallet on the pavement, not fifty yards up the road from our house. I picked it up and, without looking inside it, I took it home to my father. He glanced inside and made a show of checking the cards. But, when he thought I wasn't looking, he took a slim fold of notes from the back of the wallet and stashed them into his trouser pocket.

'Dad?'

'Kid?' He raised his eyebrow. At the age of nine, this felt like a challenge.

'Nothing,' I said, then went back to my business of identifying flowers along the roadside, which probably felt more important to me at the time anyway.

At heart, I'm an honest person, yes. But I've never been especially big on confrontation. One of the reasons this is one of my earliest memories is that my parents spent the majority of my formative years arguing with each other – not over me, I hasten to add. I was never a troublesome child – at least, not that they were aware of. But over pretty much everything else there was to argue about.

'Did you pay the water bill?'

'What do you mean you didn't get beef?'

'How are you breathing so damn loud?'

Minor issues, really, in the grand scheme of things. But it doesn't take a therapist to work out that the issues they were arguing over probably weren't *really* the issues they were arguing over. It did take a therapist to reassure me it wasn't unusual that I couldn't remember it all though. The first time I relayed my pick-and-mix childhood to a counsellor – at some point during my three years at university, when well-being is shoved down your throat – I asked whether it was normal, to have misplaced these things so easily.

'What is normal?' she asked.

I hate people answering a question with a question. But I said, as plainly as I could, 'Being able to hold on to your childhood memories, for a start.'

She laughed. 'They're unpleasant though. Why would you want to hold on to them?'

'Is that how it works?'

'Sometimes.' She made a note of something. 'Do you remember everything bad that's ever happened to you?'

It felt like a trick question. 'I mean, how would I know?'

'Okay, do you remember everything good?'

'No, I suppose not. How could I?'

'So, with this limited filing system available to our brains, why would we use that space up by holding on to memories that are bad, when we don't even have enough space for memories that are good?'

It didn't seem like the most sophisticated explanation for the human psyche I'd ever come across, but it sort of made some sense. For the years after that, I never thought there was anything strange in misplacing things that didn't fit inside the proverbial filing system of my mind. Argument with a friend? No, thank you. An exam grade I wasn't happy with? Absolutely not. Being fired from a job? Eesh, pass.

There's a problem with that though.

See, at heart, I'm an honest person. But I'm not exactly the most reliable...

WORK

No one likes their job. That's a hill I will die on.

I've worked at Rebel Press Publishing for nearly three years and the percentage of enjoyment versus utter misery I've experienced is shocking. Like most people, I fell into one job after another with my shiny degree that had little to no worth in a world where everyone has shiny degrees. There have been a lot of jobs along the way to get here, too, none of which I especially enjoyed. But here at least I've got something I'm good at, no matter my distaste: Social Media Manager. That's right, I spend my entire day on Facebook and Twitter. On days when I'm feeling especially adventurous, I'll fire up Photoshop and make a bunch of beautiful images that fit perfectly into a square shape. I'm typically given a boatload of appropriate quotes to sample from, whether they're from reviewers or novels we're about to publish. I say 'we' like I'm in any way included here. But after three years of employment everyone still calls me–

'M, I didn't realise you were in today?' Wendy's one of the best-known literary agents at Rebel Press and tries her damn hardest to be on good terms with me. Not because she actually likes me, I hasten to add, but more because she wants me to prioritise her press files over the press files of every other agent, and every other author. So when she said she didn't realise I was in, what she really meant was, 'Did you have a chance to look over those templates I sent to you? For the new Black publication? No worries, if not.' She never means no worries.

'Ah, do you know, they're on my list.'

She smiled. 'Whereabouts on the list?'

'Third down, I'd say.'

'You're a dream. Thanks, M.'

That's me: M. Pronounced Em, but in emails I'm only ever afforded the one letter rather than two. When I first joined the firm, it was assumed that my position was a temporary one. So unimportant was the role of social media, the old editor assumed he'd be able to shuffle my workload on to someone else's pile eventually, or – a drastic thought – perhaps even get the writers to do their own promotion (an idea that was laughed out the door by the agents). Because he thought my role was temporary, he never went to the trouble of learning my name. What he did do, though, whenever he addressed me directly, was start sentences with–

'Um, is that something that can be pushed through Twitter, more so?'

'Mm, can I grab you for a minute later?'

'Ahm, is there any way the images can be made into banners?'

It soon caught on. Outside of work, the friends I told thought it was more hilarious, rather than insulting, so eventually they also dropped my actual name to an initial that doesn't belong to me. Being stripped of my actual name in favour of a forced one was quite a humbling experience for me, though, as a person of privilege, so I tried to take a positive from it all. Plus, the office was full of intolerable tossers and the less they knew about me the better.

'M, are you coming to the meeting in Room A?' Beverley peered over my monitor.

'Oh, I–'

'Bev, M isn't on the rota for it,' Johnathan said, narrowing his eyes at his colleague.

'What's the meeting for?' I asked.

'It's about Eleanor's plans for the Patis series of books. Which I don't think you're working on?' Jonathan asked, his tone cutting. 'Or have the two of you made up?'

'Not that I'm aware,' I replied. I flashed him a tight smile and looked back at my monitor. Shortly after, the way they always do, they drifted away. They took a whisper of gossip along with them as they wandered down the corridor behind me. There's a certain smell, I think, to speculation and idle chatter. That's why you can always tell a newsmonger on a first glance, in my experience. They're the Beverleys and the Susans in any office.

'You're not working the Patis series then?' Susan asked as she breezed past my desk but didn't wait for a reply. I assumed because the answer was fucking obvious.

It was two hours later when a flurry of people walked past my desk again, signalling the end of the meeting. People chattered on their way and I caught the arse ends of their conversations – 'No one really knows what happened...' and 'Oh please, like you can just ask Eleanor something...' – which fuelled a personal paranoia that they might be discussing my dealings with the literary agent in question. These worries were matched only by the fear that they might not be talking about me at all. Who could possibly say which option was preferable?

When the stampede had finished, leaving the dust of hurried feet in their wake, I locked my computer and pushed away from my desk. As they'd all gone hurrying in one direction, I grabbed my water bottle and headed in the other. There was a water-and-coffee station on the way to the meeting rooms, which I thought would be a safe bet. There weren't any spaces booked out for the afternoon; I'd already checked. Let it not be said that I didn't at least try to keep out of people's ways.

I unscrewed my bottle as I walked, head down, which meant I had no idea I was about to bump into–

'Jesus Christ, don't you look–' Eleanor locked eyes with me. 'Oh, of course you don't.'

'I'm sorry, Eleanor. I was unscrewing–'

'Screws being loose is kind of your thing then, isn't it?'

As scathing comebacks go, it wasn't her best work. She sidestepped me then, still brushing away warm coffee from the edges of her blouse.

'I just didn't see you,' I said to her retreating back. 'How are things going for the Patis series of books? Is Keith doing everything you need?' It felt snivelling and a tad pathetic. But you can't blend into a place if people actively dislike you.

Eleanor turned. 'Are you offering to help?'

'If you need me. I know Keith isn't always great at the social media stuff.' *On account of it not being his damn job and all*, I thought, but didn't say, so points for me. 'He's good with the more technical stuff but for actual posts it can help to have a formal schedule.'

She considered my offer for longer than I expected her to, then said, 'Is this you trying to make up with me?'

I shrugged. 'Is that the effect it's having?'

Eleanor smiled like I was flirting with her; one side of her mouth tucked higher than the other, her eyes cast downwards in a way that might be coy. She tucked her hair behind her ears and took a hard look at me. I don't know what she saw, but it seemed to knock any coyness out of her.

'We're not square.'

'Is that a yes to my offer of help?'

'I can send over the files later this morning if that works for you,' she said, in a tone that suggested she was doing me a favour. 'I've already drawn up a schedule for when information needs to be released. The Patis series is staggered through the next eighteen months so it's a long-term project, and she's already working on the next novel.' She placed her palm against her forehead. 'I just don't know where she gets the energy for it.'

I laughed. 'Writers, hey?' But her flat expression suggested we weren't close enough to laugh about it. 'Send them over whenever you're ready and I'll add them to my list.'

'Great,' she replied, then turned to leave.

'Eleanor, about what happened...' I started, my speech dying in my throat somewhere when she shot an accusatory look at me.

'I told you already, this doesn't make us square.' She threw the rest of her sentence back at me, like scraps. 'It'll take more than a social media campaign, after what happened.'

Which would have been a fair comment, if I had any memory of what I'd done. I remember the work night out. I remember the accusations – 'You've got a nerve, talking to people like that...' – and the justifications – 'Come on, M had too much to drink and got carried away...' – and the brief disciplinary meeting with June from Human Resources – 'I understand things got out of hand with your alcohol intake at the celebration on Friday'. But beyond what I'd managed to scrapbook from colleagues, I couldn't say much. Although I could add the things I knew to be true: Eleanor didn't like me to begin with; the security guards eventually asked me to leave; and I don't drink, because of my medication.

DOCTOR

The receptionist never booked the same doctor. Because where would be the sense?

The man was old enough to be my father and he looked at me with the same disapproving stare that I recognised from my dad, too. When I walked into his examination room, I sat down without a word because he seemed like a man too busy for introductions. The only sound for the first near minute of my appointment was the stutter of his mouse wheel. He read over my notes with meticulous care and I wondered whether this was something he should have done before the appointment started; there were, after all, a lot of entries on that sheet. When he ran out of space to scroll he sighed, leaned back in his chair and looked at me face on for the first time.

'What can I do for you exactly?'

'It's a medication check-up,' I said, making a cat's cradle from my fingers in the absence of keys or jewellery to fiddle with. I hated these appointments; these ten-minute slots where someone was tasked with peering into your head to check the right amount of people were running around in there. 'I'm doing fine with the dosage, I think.'

He looked to the screen and back. '50mg, yes?' I nodded. 'We can increase it to 200mg if necessary so let's not be hasty. But we'll have a run through everything else first, shall we?' I nodded again, despite knowing the question was rhetorical. 'How do you feel in yourself, generally?' He loosened a blood pressure cuff as he asked.

'Generally, fine,' I replied, leaving out the bad feelings, as is customary.

He tucked the cuff around my arm and pulled it too tight. 'Let's see how this comes out, shall we? Keep still now, don't talk.' He hit the button to start the machine. 'Would you say your day-to-day life is manageable?' he asked and then held a finger up to pause my answer. 'In a moment.'

The cuff inflated to the point of being offensively tight, then exhaled hard all at once.

'Excellent, one hundred over seventy.' He turned to input the details. 'You mustn't be stressed, at least.' It seemed a strange assumption but I didn't correct him; he struck me as the type who wasn't exactly in the market for a life story. 'Now, temperature.' He clipped a plastic covering over his digital thermometer and wedged it into my ear. 'Your life?' he prompted.

'It's fine.'

'Manageable?'

'As much as anyone's.'

'You don't feel especially...' he petered out as my temperature registered. 'Hmm, a touch warm. Can you open wide for me, please?'

I obliged and he stuck a wooden tongue suppressor in my mouth.

'Now say aaaah for me, would you?'

'Arrrrrgh.'

'No signs of an infection there. Do you feel unwell in yourself?'

I shook my head. 'No, no signs of a cough, cold or otherwise. I haven't been struggling with the side effects that Dr Maddox mentioned either.' He narrowed his eyes at my comment. 'She said that because we were increasing my dose I might experience nausea, that sort of thing.' Which seemed like something he should know...

'Any feelings of anxiety?'

Not until a few minutes ago when someone stuck something in my mouth. 'None.'

He turned back to his computer. 'There are some weight fluctuations here, how's that looking at the moment? Do we need a weigh-in?'

I wondered whether he might lift one leg and then the other, to check for signs of lameness next.

'My weight hasn't changed since my last appointment. My appetite is fine, too.'

'Hmm.' He didn't seem convinced. 'Still, why don't you hop on the scales for me?'

I had a Body Mass Index of someone who needed to diet (me and every weightlifter around). But I had the firm mindset of someone who had no interest or intention in dieting. The doctor stood next to me while the pointer bounced back and forth between two figures. When it settled, he went to the trouble of bending over and removing his glasses, to make sure he shamed me to the pound.

'It's actually a little high at the minute,' he said, sounding smug with his correction.

'But it's historically been low.'

'Do you have plans to lose...'

I don't know what my face did, but it halted him in his tracks. 'No, I don't think it's the right time in my life for a diet.' I flashed a tight smile. 'Will my medication be available on a repeat prescription, without having to have a check-in every time?'

'How long has it been now?'

'Nearly twelve months, but three months on this current dose.'

'We'll still need to check in every six months or so, to see that you've settled with the medication.' He clicked and typed, cutting and pasting details from one part of the screen to another. 'And you're certain the dose you're on is doing the trick?'

Well, I haven't doubled over in blind panic in the centre of the high street recently, I thought but didn't say; another point for me. 'It feels like a comfortable amount for me.'

'But you'll come back if things don't feel right?' His finger hovered over the mouse button, leaving me one right answer, one click away from freedom.

'Of course.'

He clicked and placed a hand under the tray of the printer, awaiting my prescription. 'I spotted something else here, too, about your appointments elsewhere. Are you still seeing–'

I snatched the printed sheet from him. 'Yes,' I answered. 'Once every two weeks.'

FAMILY

Family members misunderstand food as love.

'You're sure you don't want a cake or anything?'

My mother was the type who ricocheted between asking me whether I'd gained weight and telling me I needed to lose it; she was old before her time like that.

'I'm fine, really. A flat white will be enough.'

Watching people in coffee shops is one of the great pastimes of the modern world, that's another hill I would die on. While Mum queued, already eyeing up the cakes I'd told her I didn't want to eat, I looked around the rest of the space. There were couples, collectives of friends, and they were all interacting with each other easily – apart from a table for two in the corner who looked like they might be breaking up, but I didn't watch. These easy interactions always chilled me, leaving me somewhere between admiration and misunderstanding; the same way that watching my GCSE Maths teacher explain an equation might have done. There was a table of women in the corner, their hair either straightened or curled to perfection, their teeth pearl white, their handbags worth more than my mortgage each month. I saw them laugh and joke and nudge each other affectionately. And, in a wistful way that wasn't entirely unfamiliar to me, I thought–

'They didn't have any trays so I've got to go back for the cake.'

Mum shakily set down two cups of coffee. Hers was a latte – the closest she could get to not actually drinking a coffee – while mine was the flat white I'd asked for, complete with a distorted stencil on top. Whoever had gone to the trouble of the design looked to have made a heart, but it had got broken on the way to me. *And doesn't that kind of say it all*, I thought as I dunked a spoon in to stir away what was left of the image. Seconds later Mum returned with a slab of lemon drizzle cake that she strategically placed on the table between us; two forks.

'How have you been, Mum, what have I missed?'

She gave me a sad smile. 'Philip and I have decided to part ways, so that's a bit of bad news. We both agreed it's for the best, though, in the long run.'

When she said we both agreed to part ways, what she meant was, 'Philip left.' Mum had developed this code for boyfriends who had decided enough was enough. In the six years since my parents' divorce, they'd both done excellent jobs of adopting their respective stereotypes: 'the jilted woman who tries too hard to find a replacement love' and 'the man who moved on at breakneck speed'. Dad walked into a new relationship suspiciously quickly for someone who claimed not to have been having an affair. Meanwhile, Mum walked in and out of many relationships but there's nothing suspicious about that; she'd been looking for her old life in a new man since her and Dad 'agreed it was for the best' for them to 'part ways'.

'That's a real shame. Neither of you have got someone else, have you?' I asked because I was feeling especially cruel. This wasn't the first or last time to have this conversation, and I reasoned I could be kind the next time around.

She shook her head. 'Well, I certainly haven't.'

'I'm sure he hasn't either,' I said, but she looked doubtful. 'Even if he has, you're better out of it, Mum. There's no sense in being with someone who isn't committed.' I paused for a sip of coffee, and to give her the time to mull over the platitude. 'How's everything else?' There wasn't really anything else for her to talk about, I knew that much. But I wasn't prepared for her break-up with Philip to be the only topic of conversation.

'Work's going well. There's a promotion going for higher up in the sales department, so I'm hoping that I'll get a look in for that. I've been talking to the girls a lot more, too, since Philip.' Her voice cracked over his name and she took three hard blinks, as though steadying tears. It looked like she really was grieving – for something. But really, Philip? 'They've mentioned having a little weekend away somewhere, the lot of us, which I think would be nice. Haven't done something like that since I was with your father.' *Oh*, I thought, *here comes the turn in conversation.* 'Have you spoken to him much recently?'

Dad and I had a touch-and-go relationship, even when I was knee-high in age. After the incident with the wallet, I never quite looked at him in the same way. I think there's a moment in everyone's lives when you realise that your parents – while still being your parents, sure – are also just people, with flaws and shitty morals, just like the next person you'd meet on the street. Flaws and shitty morals were something that Dad had always had in abundance, I later learned. He treated Mum like a doormat throughout their divorce and, when the paperwork came through, I remember a distinct feeling that he'd somehow legally separated from the both of us.

'We don't really talk that much these days, Mum.' We didn't talk that much, no, but we did try to have breakfast, lunch or dinner with each other once a month. It wasn't for me, though, it was for his good lady who he 'didn't leave his marriage for' (that old chestnut). He'd managed to stay with her all these years, and she liked to see him making an effort with me. I wasn't stupid enough to let Mum find out about that though. 'I'll call him in a couple of weeks, make sure he's still alive and stuff.'

She half-laughed. 'He still with what's-her-name?'

Mum knew her name, but it wouldn't suit the stereotype if she brought herself to say it out loud. 'He was when we last talked, sure. They're fine, settled.' I sipped. 'But it's been a few weeks since we talked so he could be back on the market by now.'

'Well, someone else is free to buy him then,' she said, her mouth downturned as though I'd suggested a lewd act. Maybe getting back with your ex-husband was considered lewd by the time you were their age.

'Work's going well for me too,' I said, sensing a point for a subject change. 'I've had a lot of big campaigns dropped on my desk lately, including one from Eleanor.'

'You two are talking again?'

'That might be a stretch, but she didn't throw her drink over me.'

Mum looked uncomfortable at the mention of Eleanor, whenever I brought her up. The first time had been immediately after the incident – whatever the incident had been. In the months since, I'd tried to explain to Mum that I sincerely couldn't remember what I'd done to cause offence, and she'd always said something like–

'People forgive eventually, don't they?'

'Sure.' I drained the remains of my coffee.

'Another?'

'Actually,' I looked at my watch, 'I should think about getting off.'

'But we haven't even got to the good stuff,' she said, finally reaching for one of the forks between us. She cut herself a piece of cake and spoke through a spray of crumbs, 'You've told me about work, how about the personal life? What have I missed?' I narrowed my eyes. 'Come on, a mother can't ask about their own offspring's love life? You're an only child and I want me some grandchildren. Isn't there someone special, a special...' she petered out around the point where a pronoun should be. Having never brought a prospective partner home to my family, they'd always been stumped on which sex I preferred to sex.

This was, I thought, Mum's attempt to live vicariously through me. She did this sometimes, when things weren't great with her own life; maybe it's something all parents lean towards. Either way, she was chomping at the bit to know something – anything.

'I'm sort of seeing someone.'

She squealed; a girly squeal that belonged to someone a third of her age. 'Who?'

'Mum, I really don't want to talk about this yet.'

'Oh, oh, I see.' She swallowed another wedge of cake. 'Early days?'

Not really. 'Kind of. Look, it's just someone I'm seeing. Can we not make a thing?'

She huffed. 'Okay, well, can you at least tell me when you're next seeing this someone?'

'Later this week.' I started to collect my things; the universal signal for, can I fuck off and leave now? 'It's nothing set in stone. We're both busy people. But I might see them in a couple of days' time, for dinner.' Which wasn't a lie.

DINNER

There are some things that never lose their novelty.

I had certain outfits reserved for special occasions: visiting distant family; having a night out with friends; having dinner in with someone who I deem to be extraordinary. Which is why, three days after this blessed conversation with Mum, I came home from work and spent forty minutes in front of my bedroom mirror, trying on different outfits. One after the other, I went from demure to outright slutty in a button-down shirt that revealed more chest than any self-respecting person should show – fortunately for me, I had no such respect. But I eventually decided on tight but not uncomfortable jeans and a plain black T-shirt, tucked in, because showing a toned shape has never been anyone's worst idea for a date night. That said, this wasn't the first dinner date, and we'd likely moved past the point of me needing to wear something difficult but enhancing. Comfortable and enhancing would be fine.

The cooking itself wasn't anything sophisticated; a leg of lamb surrounded by vegetables ready to roast, the whole thing could be wedged into the oven and left. The perk of this was obvious – who actually enjoyed cooking? – but there were drawbacks, too, namely that I had nothing to distract myself with. Oh, but I tried.

While the oven hummed and clicked in the background, I set about rearranging the furniture in my living room-dining room. The two rooms were conjoined, and the open plan allowed me to breathe a little easier. But there were certain adjustments that needed to be made for home dinner dates. I pushed the sofa back until it sat against one wall and repeated the process for the armchair opposite. The coffee table I moved into what was essentially the dining area itself. My dining table wasn't big – big enough to sit four people, that is, but not big enough to induce feelings of loneliness. I dragged it from its usual spot and pretended to ignore the grate of wood against laminate flooring – the damage was done, I reasoned, but the sound was deafening. It quietened when the furniture was in the centre of the room. I walked to the other side and pushed, trying a different tactic, until the table was wedged under the window ledge. I pulled up a chair and tucked it in, just in time for the oven to ding.

The lamb needed extra seasoning and the vegetables needed more oil. But soon the clang of metal on metal, and the thud of the oven door closing all reminded me of one missing ingredient.

'Music.' I pulled out my phone and loaded up the playlist I'd reserved for these occasions. 'Music sets the tone for everything.' The speaker crackled as the first song came to life. Back in the dining area for the night, I left my phone on the sideboard to work through a list of date-appropriate songs.

'Girl, something, something, giiiirl, sometimes...'

I sang along to the Guns N' Roses track on my walk back to the kitchen. The song shook loose a half memory of something. Middle school? Most likely. I was part of a friendship group that still thought old rock music was the height of style. We were a lively bunch back then, before age and work and mortgage payments caught up with us. But I couldn't place the specifics of how we all broke apart.

In the kitchen, I pulled out crockery, cutlery and a serving dish; the latter, I left on the work surface for the lamb. Carole King crooned an accompaniment on my walk back to the living room where I laid the table. I liked to make an effort with these things; these early days felt especially important.

For an evening that had felt slow, by the time King's vocals were coming to an end the alarm on my phone trilled an excited announcement to let me know it was nearly time. With the playlist on shuffle, Taylor Swift's upbeat vocals carried me through pulling the lamb from the oven and plating it, half dancing the entire time. So at least my nerves hadn't fully arrived.

The living room was a picture of romance. The playlist skipped on to Coldplay as I set the food on the table and took my seat. I'd left the chair on the outer side, opposite the window itself. Then I spooned vegetables onto my plate, cut the meat and served a decent portion (it had been a long day, I deserved this). The potatoes hadn't softened as much as I liked them to, but the flavour of everything combined was something beautiful. Midway through those first mouthfuls, I looked up in time to catch the light going on in the apartment opposite – a mirrored layout to mine. He came in, already loosening the tie from his shirt, and I watched.

HIM

There are times in life when things just get out of hand.

Caleb moved into the building opposite mine six months ago. I walked past when the van was unloading. 'Apartment nineteen,' he said, 'it's marked Caleb Neale on the buzzer already.' The information was there, readily available for anyone who happened to be walking by at the time. There were boxes of books, hangers of clothes and beautiful pieces of furniture packed into the back of the loading truck – and I was curious.

For the first couple of weeks I watched as he arranged and rearranged the mirrored apartment. All of these blocks were built the same, so his living room window was opposite my own – as was his dining room window, although he soon made that a home office space. Not that he worked from home all the time. His workdays, I later learned, were mostly spent at one of the swanky offices right in the centre of the city. We walked to work together one day – unbeknownst to him, and I tried not to make a habit of doing that more than once every few weeks because there had to be a limit. His home life was where my attention was focused.

In his living room he set up a leather sofa, surrounded by heavy pieces of wooden furniture – which was my first clue that Caleb lived alone. He soon made friends with the local food delivery drivers too – which was another clue – but he wasn't afraid of cooking. I often watched him, while I ate my own dinner sometimes, as he walked into his living room shovelling something home-cooked into his mouth. He'd land heavily on the sofa and continue eating like no one was watching. There were even times when he'd leave the dirty plate right there on the sofa next to him – and that was another clue that he lived by himself.

The first few weeks were spent watching him decide between paint swatches – he made the wrong call for the living room, I think, but everyone has their preferences. He continued to rearrange furniture which made me wonder whether this was his first home; or, more specifically, whether this was his first home alone. I imagined him, having separated from a controlling partner, now embracing a homeowner's freedom to have a feature wall painted in dark teal (even though it made the room smaller) and to leave dirty plates on the floor of the living room (all so you can put your feet up for half an hour before bed and then leave the plate behind until the following day). These imagined specifics unfolded the more I watched him. But I wanted the facts too.

I'd had a bad week at work, and from the amount of time Caleb had spent on the phone, pacing from one room to another, I assumed it hadn't been a great week for him either. I watched him stand in front of a mirror fixed to the back living room wall, tweaking his hair and buttoning, unbuttoning, buttoning the top two buttons on his shirt – and I was curious, still. When he left the house I grabbed my keys, phone and wallet, and then left along with him. It was idle wonder that carried me four steps behind Caleb the whole way back into town and to a gastropub that might otherwise have been too stylish for me to visit. I perched at the bar and treated myself to a lemonade with a twist of lime. Caleb was two humans away from me ordering his own drink. Then he turned and searched for his tribe.

'We thought you'd forgotten us, lad!' one bellowed, slapping Caleb on the shoulder.

'Friday night drinks? Never.'

'What you on?' another asked.

'Vodka tonic.'

'Ooh,' another two chimed in synchronicity.

'What can I say, I'm gender neutral for drinks,' Caleb said, laughing along with them.

It was the first time I'd even noticed him leaving the house on a Friday. But the longer I watched, the more I saw this was a regular occurrence for him. Every Friday he repeated the procedure of tweaking his hair, buttoning, unbuttoning, and buttoning his shirt, and stumbling in six hours later. There were some Saturday mornings where it was clear he hadn't made it to bed at all; some Saturday mornings, though, it was clear he hadn't made it to bed alone.

I wouldn't have called Caleb a Lothario. In six months he'd brought home a small selection of one-night stands, all of whom got breakfast and a kiss on the cheek the following morning. But most of his attention lay with his Tuesday girl.

Tuesday arrives at the same time every week and she always brings takeout with her. She sometimes brings pizza, sometimes Chinese; whatever the dish, they sit on the sofa together and eat it right there from the containers like they're animals – or, rather, like they're close friends. They laugh and joke and eat and then they have sex right there on the leather seats, in full view of anyone who might be watching – which I suspect isn't something they've thought about (although people have their preferences). Tuesday doesn't stay overnight to Wednesday morning, but they always leave on affectionate terms – her terms, though, not his. Caleb often looks to be gently pulling her back into the living room whenever she heads for the door. But she's kind when she leaves, giving him a kiss on the cheek or a soft poke on the nose, as though they really are emotionally attached to each other. He's always deflated after she's gone; I see his whole body shrug. He's gentleman enough to wipe down the sofa when they've finished, though, which I hadn't expected. Although given that the one-nighters never usually make it to the bedroom, it's probably safer sex for everyone if antibacterial wipes are involved.

The small trail of beautiful women led in and out of the flat are how I know I'm not Caleb's type – and believe me, if you look at the carbon copies he's sleeping with, I'm certain they're a type. Even the harmless social media browsing I did didn't reveal any changes in preferences, based on profile pictures from 2013 at least, which is the last time he shared a square with another human face. There was a dog pictured with him once that I tried to find mention of elsewhere – I was curiouser still. But there was never another mention of the dog. One or two bitches pictured, maybe, but never the dog.

About a month into Caleb living in the apartment, I found out he comes from a two-parent household. A mother figure and a father figure eventually turned up and took a good look around the place, and his mother set a hand flat against the teal feature wall in the living room. I had no idea what she said, of course, but she didn't look impressed. Caleb gave up his bed for the best part of a week during their visit. He folded the leather seats out into something that resembled a sofa-bed, and I watched him, lit up by an overbearing full moon, toss and turn as he tried to get comfortable. He did this every evening they were there – as though he expected the makeshift bed to have got more comfortable over the day – apart from Tuesday's evening. She didn't come over – which said a lot, I thought – but I think she called. It was late when I saw his handset light up the darkened room; the space otherwise only lit by a salt lamp. I saw him smile and laugh and then I saw him get up, hold the phone away from his ear and listen from the doorway of the dining room, as though checking for signs of life elsewhere. He pulled the dining room door closed and crept back to bed, phone still pressed to his ear. Then he talked for a while longer before leaning back and reaching a hand under the creased sheets. He moved slowly up and down himself, head tipped back – and, curious, I watched.

FRIENDS

There are some things you just can't do with other friends.

'What do you think of them, first date or second?'

Mary and I met in our second year of university thanks to a cock-up in the student housing department. We were thrust together in a shared flat when we'd both requested single-person accommodation. But our shared distaste of other people was the very thing that caused us to bond that year. After that, we made a concerted effort to stay in touch (something neither of us did all that often with others) and part of that effort had always involved dinner out together at least once a month – all so we could judge, and watch.

'It's got to be their first. Blind date, too, I'd say.'

Mary shot me a look. 'How in the hell can you possibly know that?'

'She's wearing flat shoes.' Mary looked back at the couple, focusing on the woman's feet. 'What woman does that if she knows she's coming to a restaurant on a Saturday night?'

'I'm wearing flat shoes.'

'Is this a date?' I raised an eyebrow and smiled. 'Because if you want this to be a da–'

'Okay, joker,' she interrupted me, 'you've made your point.'

The waiter appeared with our pizza-for-two that took up the majority of the table. It left just enough room for our small plates either side, but Mary handed them back to the young man – 'We won't be needing those.' – instead going straight to the pizza cutter. She and I didn't exactly stand on ceremony for each other.

'So I'm thinking of moving,' she announced, mid-cut.

'To where?'

'Glasgow.'

'*The* Glasgow?'

She looked up at me. 'Is there another one?'

'I'm hoping so.'

'Come on, don't be funny.'

'I'm not laughing.' I took the rugged slice of pizza that she'd half cut, half ripped away from the main body of food. 'Why on earth would you move there?'

'For a fresh start,' she said, poised to take a mouthful of her own slice.

'What kind of a bullshit answer is that? A fresh start from what?' I lowered my voice. 'Mare, have you killed someone? Because that's no reason to leave the city, we can take care of that sort of situation between the two of–'

'Oh, look at you, funny again,' she said through her food. 'Don't you ever get tired?'

'Yeah, Mare, but I take a nap.'

'Not that kind of tired.'

I swallowed my mouthful. 'Then no, I don't get tired.'

She set her food down and huffed. 'I'm just considering it, that's all. There's nothing set in stone. It wouldn't be soon-soon if I went, because I'd need to sell the flat, and look for work up there.' She paused. 'Not necessarily in that order. But there are things I'd need to get done before I left. Anyway, I just thought I'd float it.'

'Have you floated it with anyone else?'

'Just you.'

'Talk to some others about it.'

'Why?'

I wiped my mouth clean of tomato sauce. 'So they can tell you what a fucking daft idea it is. Waiter, can I get a lemonade with a twist of lime over here?'

Mary laughed. 'Something to steady your nerves.'

'What can I say, I'm shaken.'

There are some friends who I meet for things like eating pizza; people-watching and work-moaning; family comparisons and memory-lane trips (although the latter doesn't happen that often). Then there are some friends who I watch with their friends. They don't exactly see me. But I see them.

There are times in life when I – as a creature of habit – have bumped into another – also a creature of habit – while doing our habitual things. That's how it starts. During a midday visit to a coffee shop with Mum, many moons ago, I noticed faces that I'd somehow noticed before. My memory had never been great, so placing people was sometimes a hard task. Instead, I watched them for a while – one Saturday after another. I took a magazine and slowly flipped through pages, making a show of reading. When really, I was watching Blonde talk to Brunette in hushed tones, as though bad-mouthing someone, and when Red came back from the counter they promptly stopped their conversation and launched into another. I watched Dad talk to Daughter in a condescending tone – 'You aren't to burden your mother with this, do you understand?' – and listened in as Daughter snapped back – 'Because you don't want her to know what a bastard you are, is that it?' – making no effort to keep her tones hushed. But when I saw them the following week, Daughter and Dad seemed to have made up; meanwhile, it was Blonde and Red who were talking about Brunette, up until she took her seat at the table. They were once joined by Blonde Two but she only came the one time and I wondered whether it had been some kind of initiation to see whether she could be a part of the group. Whatever the task, she'd failed.

'Come on, we need to eat lunch.'

I didn't recognise his voice, having only heard it during snatched conversations. But I recognised his figure as soon as Caleb sat down, only three tables away, with a man of a similar age to him. Caleb scanned the chalkboard menus around the space while his friend flipped through something on his phone.

'What are you doing?'

The Friend looked up. 'Tinder.'

'Right now? While I'm sitting right here?'

'You're surprised?'

'No, I'm hungry.' Caleb looked back at the boards. 'Are you eating anything, or do you just want a camomile tea?'

'Camomile tea?'

'You know, to chill you the fuck out.' Caleb's tone was jovial but his friend didn't look impressed. He reached over the table to knock the phone out of his comrade's hand. 'Have a drink and something to eat, and we can get back to it then.'

The Friend let out a hard sigh. 'I'm just bloody bored of ring shopping.'

'Then put a Hula Hoop on her finger.' Caleb stood. 'Food or no?'

'Get me a cheese toastie.'

The bell hanging over the door – a weak attempt at making the place seem quaint – rang to signal the entry of another couple I recognised. Regulars – Tired and Ms Tired – came in mid-argument, as they often did. They argued over where to sit, then over whether they were eating, over what to drink – 'Do you really feel like you need caffeine right now, while you're breastfeeding still?' he snapped, but didn't wait for an answer. This was the first time I'd heard a baby mentioned, but it made sense.

'She's such a bitch.'

'Mum and I aren't really talking.'

'Do we have to go out drinking every weekend?'

I listened to a collage of conversations and tried to make mental notes. It wasn't that being around other people was hard. But from the earliest memories of my childhood friendships through to the adult ones, it always felt like something was – blank.

'They're bringing the food over.' Caleb sat back down at his table. 'Still on Tinder?'

'Nah, I'm texting Sally to tell her we're having lunch.'

'She want to join us?'

The Friend huffed out a laugh. 'To go ring shopping for my other woman? I doubt it.'

I tried hard not to judge Caleb by the company he kept. But he didn't make it easy.

'Do you mind me grabbing that chair?'

Ms Tired snapped me out of my concentration.

'Not at all, feel free.'

'Thanks.'

She carried the seat back to her own table where her husband was waiting with three drinks. They were bunched together on a bench seat, closer than I'd ever seen them, and the chair was opposite. I watched, on and off, for nearly five minutes until a woman much younger than them came in and took a quick scan of the crowd. She soon spotted them and approached with a warm smile and an extended hand – one that Tired was a little too eager to shake. Ms Tired looked like she'd noticed this too.

'Why get engaged at all?'

'Can we invite her along one week, out of curiosity?'

'We don't drink every weekend. You're being dramatic there.'

People have often recommended this kind of learning through observation. The trips to the coffee shop have always felt like my hour of personal development then, to learn people and try to understand – but mostly to watch.

STAFF MEETING

S ocial media is a cesspit for the modern age.

On the walk from the entry doors to my desk I heard six different people use the phrase 'status update' in a sentence. They're the main means of communication. People don't tell each other anything personally, but they do make a public show of it by writing it across a colour block and posting it to every channel they can think of.

I landed hard in my chair and switched my computer on.

For anyone working in social media, having such a disdain for it could be problematic.

I keyed in my password and my personal desktop started to unfold.

But, again, no one really likes their job, and everyone needs something to keep lamb on the table and a dim-watt bulb on at night.

There were thirty-one emails waiting for me in my inbox. I decided to strategically start with Eleanor's. To say that her tone was pleasant was stretching the truth but she'd afforded me the luxury of a personal sign-off – *Thanks again, Eleanor* – rather than her standard email signature, which must have taken a lot of effort. Since we'd talked earlier there had been a steady stream of information from her regarding the Patis publications. Eleanor had said there was a schedule in place for when information needed to be released but it was a sliding door schedule, changing every few hours some days. In truth, it was a fucking nightmare already but if it was a ticket to smoothing over some status in the office then it would be worth it.

'Are you coming to the meeting?' Jonathan peered over my monitor. Hannah, Beverley and Dotty were clustered behind him, like groupies – or cult members. Jonathan always had status; he was the type for it.

'What meeting?'

Hannah coughed softly. 'The staff meeting.'

Jonathan cast a look back at her but I couldn't see his expression. When he faced me again he flashed a fake smile. 'It's staff meeting day.'

'Staff meetings are on Fridays,' I replied.

'Which today is.'

I looked at my desk calendar. Thursday had been crossed out, but I couldn't...

'I'm just going to grab a drink,' I said. 'I'll be right down.'

This seemed to pacify the gaggle. 'Come on then, goslings.' Jonathan clapped as he walked, and the women followed. I didn't know whether it was a pop culture reference or a comment on their clucking.

I went to the drink station and half-filled a cup with cold water. It wasn't often that I had to take extra tablets, but I had a lower dosage for when the days were too long, or the noise was too loud, or my brain was too full of nonsense. Back at my desk I broke a tablet free of its silver sleeve and threw it back with the water. It should kick in midway through the meeting – that I was now definitely late for.

There was a steady stream of people entering the room still, so I snuck in unnoticed – which seemed to sum up my existence in the office. The lead agents were talking in hurried tones as though they were panicked about their work, but I realised a long time ago that this was how busy people talked to each other. The editors talked like it, too, commenting on inconsistencies and formatting software as though there were gun barrels fixed to the backs of their heads, demanding they spill. The publishing director took on a softer tone – Gladis Swan, her actual name, apparently – and she encouraged others to do the same, but it never did stick.

'Um,' she started, and I looked up out of habit. There was a giggle from somewhere alongside me as though someone had noticed my stand to attention, but I couldn't work out who. 'So, could we have an update on the Nicholl contract?'

Fred piped up for this one. 'He's signed!' There was a jovial cheer around the office. 'At long last, we've managed to grab him. We've locked him in for a two-book contract with a mind to extend the contract for further publications.'

'Who is it that negotiated the two books rather than more?' Gladis asked.

'He did, but he also said he's happy to be working with us for the time being.'

'Not happy enough to sign a five-book deal though,' Eleanor said, loud enough for the cheap seats at the back to hear the comment. 'Still, well done, Fred, that's a great feat.'

'It is,' Gladis added, her tone firmer. 'We should celebrate. The lot of us.' She looked around the room to gauge a reaction from the faces. 'Drinks tonight? It's Friday after all and who doesn't deserve a gin at the end of – well, any day of the week.' She laughed and the room – or most of the room – laughed along with her. 'I'll send a poll.' She liked us to believe work was a democracy.

In the seconds that followed, someone muttered, 'Um.' It

was Eleanor this time. My head snapped up like a knee-jerk reaction, and she laughed. She'd been watching for it. 'Sorry, it escapes me now what I was going to say,' she finished.

Gladis looked my way but she didn't intervene. 'Okay, so to wrap up...'

By mid-afternoon the office had established that drinks on that particular Friday night weren't going to work – by the grace of God. The poll gave us next week as an option instead which the majority of my co-workers had voted for so, not one to buck the trend, I hit that date as well. Planning these things a week in advance made it easier for me to prepare for – emotionally, intellectually, spiritually and the rest of it. Drinks with work people was never as fun as people expected it to be, and I had a track record of getting stressed in situations like this. The sheer commitment of adding the date to my work diary had me reaching for the silver strip of pills in my bag. If it weren't for the one I'd already taken – and the drowsy effects of it – I would have treated myself to another. But somehow falling asleep at my desk on a sunny Friday afternoon didn't seem like something that would go down all that well – or go unnoticed.

I went to grab one final coffee for the day and bumped into Beverley, waiting for an extra shot to pour into her takeout cup. So I wasn't the only one in need of a nap on the company's time.

She laughed. 'Fridays, right?'

'Christ, tell me about it.'

Beverley and I had never been friendly, but we didn't have an active dislike of each other either.

'I noticed you're going to the drinks next Friday?' she asked, fixing the lid to her drink.

Lord, here we go, I thought. But I swallowed, smiled and said, 'Planning on it.'

'Well, try to behave yourself this time, won't you?' She winked as though that would soften the blow of the comment, and then stepped out of my way. 'Toodles.'

I grabbed a paper cup, wedged it into the dispenser and hit the button for a flat white. When the machine groaned into life I turned and looked along the corridor that Beverley had disappeared down. She stopped at every other desk along the way, saying hello to those who were sticking it out and goodbye to those who had given up on Friday early. I saw her throw a sly look behind her before she rounded the corner to her own workspace, as though to check whether I was watching – but of course I was.

RESEARCH

Every cesspit has it uses.

My social media accounts exist, and have always existed, because people expect them to. I've never fooled myself into believing my life is anywhere near interesting enough for other people to want a look into it. But, it turns out, if you aren't on social media at all then people assume you're doing something worth noticing – which I'm not, I just don't like to be watched. Still, I posted the occasional tweet and updated my status accordingly every Friday or Saturday – '*Geez, what a week – feeling exhausted*' – and sometimes, when I was feeling especially adventurous, I'd post a picture to my Instagram feed. It was usually of food, occasionally of books (very occasionally, but at least the food looked good).

The main attraction for social media is that it allows us to see people. Although for some the main attraction is that it allows them to be seen.

Alcohol never agreed with me – it always made me lose too much time – but the taste of non-alcoholic wine was a lot to give up. It was earlier than I'd usually open a bottle, but late-morning one Saturday I cracked the seal and poured myself a generous measure of something fruity and zesty, and I grabbed my laptop. When I typed 'find' into the search bar, Caleb's profile came up before my own. I allowed myself this time, just one hour a week because otherwise I can become compulsive and that was something I needed to avoid. His profile unfolded and I opened a fresh window to check his other accounts too.

Instagram was the liveliest from the night before. He'd come home late – I hadn't needed a social media update to tell me that; I'd seen the lights go on – but the feed was full of pictures of where he'd been. His stories were made up of flickering lights and tone-deaf singing, shouted into the speaker by his drunken comrades. There were still images of them in among the video stream; Caleb holding the phone as far away from them as possible, to get four, five, six people into the picture frame. His eyes weren't focused, and I wondered how he'd managed to take the pictures at all. *Christ, you're a mess when you're drunk*, I thought, clicking from one update to another. There weren't any photos uploaded to his profile, though, so no matter the fun he'd been having it hadn't been a night he'd wanted people to see forever.

I watched the last of his videos and closed the window, replacing it with Twitter. He only really used it for work updates and without more context it was hard to get much use from them. Some comments about late nights at the office (which mostly weren't true) and a few tags for local businesses he'd visited.

'How do I find out what you do, Caleb?' I took a final gulp of wine to empty the glass. 'More wine, sir, certainly more wine.' Surprisingly, Caleb didn't have a LinkedIn account, and the information he'd shared on Facebook didn't pertain to his work life.

I poured another generous measure and went back into the living room.

It was clever of him, really, to avoid people finding him. Anyone who he met through work might naturally search for people associated with the company but without the information listed...

'Hmm, clever.'

Twitter gave me one thing of interest though: '*Excellent meal at @workurbuns. Looking forward to a repeat next Thursday.*'

I flicked to the next week in my diary and starred the date, adding a 'C' alongside it. There was nothing to be done, obviously, but it was nice to keep track of these things. Seeing Caleb come home full or tipsy or tired – sometimes all three – was entertainment enough. The poor television in my living room had seen limited action in the last six months thanks to Caleb's openness with his status updates.

He also had a nasty (for him) habit of sharing events that he was going to via Facebook. I closed the Twitter window and went back to my first choice. There wasn't anything shared there to explain his trip out on Thursday, so I added '*work thing?*' to my diary and went back to my browsing. I had a colour-coded system to show which were his things and mine, to try to avoid this situation getting too complicated. Although I'd considered getting a separate diary entirely, but then I'd be checking one against the other all the time – this was just more efficient. Although he had a lot of events coming up in the next two weeks...

Another of Caleb's many bad habits was checking in to places too, which is how I know where he drinks his coffee, which gym he uses, and – from pictures, not a check-in – which part of the city he walks through when he wants a good sunset view. It would have been easy to stage a run-in with Caleb and have it be completely natural and inconspicuous – but it felt like a line. On the weeks when this 'research' felt stranger than it normally does, I consoled myself greatly with the fact that a run-in had never happened. But it wasn't something I ruled out. After all, accidents happen.

The screen tipped beneath my cursor and a small bubble reading '*new posts*' appeared. I refreshed and found a new status update: '*Been looking forward to this all week – feeling relaxed at Holland's Day Spa.*'

Holland's Day Spa was a ten-minute walk away from our apartments. It would be impossible to get a last-minute appointment for myself on a Saturday...

I drained another glass of fake wine while I finished browsing through Caleb's profiles. Occasionally, I checked his picture against online search engines to see whether it would link me back to dating websites. But only when it had been an especially bad week for me. In many ways, this hour of research was my comfort food for the week – or it was some kind of binge. Like a true hobbyist, though, when I'd finished with my allotted time I closed down the windows on my screen and set the laptop to one side, then I cleared space in my mind for other things. I went back into the kitchen to fix lunch – and to see what wine options were available – and I didn't give Caleb another thought. What I was doing, I reasoned, was no different to any other hobby; stamp-collecting, or compulsively reading a series of novels. I was always waiting, watching to see what the character would do next.

BREAKFAST

Lies come in different shades of grey.

I could never bring myself to tell my mum when I had plans with my dad. It always felt like cheating on one parent with another. And in my experiences of cheating, it's always best to wait until you're backed into a corner with that sort of thing.

The dining room had been reassembled after my last 'dinner date', so it looked like a space fit for two people. I hadn't laid out the placemats or cutlery by the time my dad arrived though. He was more comfortable when he had something to do, so that became his unofficial role in breakfast while I took care of everything else. While I waited for him, I stood beating eggs into submission – omelettes, I'd decided – and rerunning everything from the evening before: the dreaded works drinks.

Despite better judgement, I'd committed to going and I'd stuck by it. I mingled with the other social media representatives and made idle chat with an editor and an agent, moving around the group strategically to make sure I covered every department. No one could say that I hadn't shown my face. Although I'd deliberately avoided the table that Eleanor and a few others had flocked to; I didn't want to push my luck.

Wendy – one of the flock – held her drink up to me and smiled, and I reciprocated by tipping my near empty lemonade back at her before moving on to my next target. She was keeping me on side because of the Black social media campaign that we were putting together. But I reasoned that flashing her a smile – maybe I should've even winked – wouldn't hurt my status in the office. After I'd hit my quota of people for the night, I drained my glass and shrugged on my coat. The other members of the social media team noticed my move and shouted their goodbyes over the growing music, and I waved in return. There were three steps between me and the doorway of the bar when someone caught my arm though. I remember turning, and seeing – Eleanor? Wendy? I remember turning, and a raised voice, and I tried to leave and–

A firm knock against my front door interrupted everything. The eggs were over-beaten, and the oven's alarm was chirping to let me know the timer was finished. When I'm tired I lose things – my keys, headphones, memory – and from kitchen to front door I managed to convince myself that's all that had happened (again). But there was a nagging feeling...

In the doorway my dad stood tall and proud, resting a hand on his belly to mark his hunger. 'I'm wasting away here,' he said, stepping over the threshold. 'Something smells good, though, kid.'

He threw his arms around me for an oversized hug. 'There are home-made hash browns and pork sausages in the oven, and I'm about to knock together a share-sized omelette.' I spoke over his shoulder. There was a time when I was so much smaller than him, but age had started to take his height. 'Don't tell Carol what I'm feeding you, though, okay?'

Dad pushed me away and held me by the shoulders at arm's length. 'Are you crazy? Carol thinks we eat spinach smoothies every time I come over here.' He let me go and stepped into the hallway behind me while I closed the door. 'Come on then, kid, feed me up.'

My dad called me kid because if he could convince himself I was in my late teens then that must mean he hadn't missed *that* much of my life. The reality was different. But we'd arrived at an amicable space where it felt rude to point out his inaccuracies.

When I joined him in the kitchen he already had his head in the fridge. 'Got juice?'

'Bottom shelf,' I replied, going back to the plasma that passed for whisked eggs. 'There's orange or cranberry.' He let out an unimpressed grunt. 'Cranberry juice is good for you. You can tell Carol you've had it.' The eggs hissed as they hit the pan. I left them to simmer while I turned the oven off behind me. 'The glasses are in the top cupboard.'

'You're always moving things.'

'You're always forgetting things.' I stirred and folded the mixture, giving every inch its chance to cook. If Carol really thought we were eating spinach, then sending my dad home with salmonella would look suspicious. 'Can you grab some cutlery for the table?'

'Jesus,' he said, but his tone was jovial. 'I come over here to be waited on and I make my own drinks, lay my own table.'

'Did you think to ask what your last slave died of?'

'I was too busy interviewing for a new one.'

He disappeared from the room with two drinks.

'Anything to report on?' he asked as he walked back in. The cutlery knocked together as he yanked the drawer open. 'Promotion, pregnancy, engagement?'

I laughed. 'All of those would be difficult for a literal boatload of reasons.'

'A father's got to ask.'

He left the room again, loaded up to set the table.

We tried to make our meetings as efficient as possible. The

breakfast was cooked, the pleasantries exchanged, and everyone could go about the rest of their month feeling like they'd done a good job at meeting a father/child. I'd realised long ago these meetings weren't to benefit either of us, but more to benefit Carol – who never even came to them, despite me asking her every time one was arranged. 'You two need your time,' she said to us both, lying through her veneers. But Carol didn't have children, and by the time she and dad met it was too late for them to try. Because of that she insisted on us having something that resembled a functioning relationship and the only way to soften that for either of us had been to involve food. Whenever we met for breakfast, Dad came to mine and I cooked. Whenever we met for lunch or dinner, I picked the restaurant and he paid; like your traditional broken home.

'What about your person,' he asked, as I tucked my chair in. 'You know, your...' he trailed off and waved his fork at me.

'Yeah, Dad, I'm still seeing them. Once a fortnight.'

'That working out for you?'

'Hard to say.' I shoved a piece of sausage into my mouth to avoid further questioning.

'Well, it's early days, I suppose.' He matched my gesture, but with a chunk of hash brown, topped with egg. He groaned as he chewed. 'Perfection, kid, per-fec-tion.'

'Thanks, Dad. Do you want tea, coffee?'

He shook his head. 'Juice is grand.'

'How are things with you anyway?'

'Well, funny story.' He set his cutlery down. It seemed to me that whenever anyone started a sentence with that, whatever was coming likely wasn't all that funny. I concentrated on eating, hoping that whatever this funny thing was it wouldn't be hilarious enough to make me choke. 'Carol and I, we've decided to get married.'

I pause mid-chew and looked up at my dad. 'Like, married, married?'

He laughed. 'No, pretend married. Yes, married, married. What other kind is there?'

'So, you proposed?'

'Sort of.' He started up eating again. 'We're both of an age where we have to make sensible decisions about our lives. Being married, from a legal point of view, just makes good sense to us both.'

'So, you had a conversation about dying, and decided it would be easier on the leftover party if you'd been married to each other?' I translated. He considered my rephrasing and then nodded enthusiastically, too busy throwing egg and sausage around his mouth to afford me a proper answer. 'But you said you'd never get married again after Mum.'

He frowned, and swallowed hard. 'I don't remember saying that.'

'Well, you did.' My dad's version of 'the talk' had been telling me to take what I needed and run before anyone mentioned wedding bands. 'You definitely said it, Dad,' I added when he didn't respond.

'Hmm.' He drained the remains of his juice and thought for a second. 'In that case, I guess I lied.'

HIM

There are times in life when a sit down with yourself is essential.

After four days of work without comments, I decided that whatever I was half-remembering from the evening couldn't have been bad. There were no hooded looks from behind monitors, and no moments of sudden silence when I caught people gossiping at the coffee station. Nor had Eleanor pulled the Patis promotional campaign from me, which was the true benchmark of bad behaviour on my part. On Thursday afternoon I took an extra tablet – I reasoned I could sleep it off when I got home, if needed – and told myself to calm down (because that's always a successful tactic for taking your panic off something). I hadn't noticed Wendy edge round the corner to my workstation as I threw my head back to swallow the pill.

'Headache?' she said, as she perched on the corner of my desk.

I made a show of rubbing my temples. 'Something like that.' When she didn't say anything more, I added, 'I'm sorry, did I miss an email?'

'Oh, no, nothing like that. I just thought I'd stick my head in to say hello. You've done some excellent work this week. The Beevis publication?' She made an okay gesture with one hand. 'The book cover really pops on that background.'

Despite her being complimentary, I couldn't help but wish that Wendy would cut to the chase. 'I can do something similar for your upcoming stuff?'

'I trust your eye, really. Do whatever feels right for it.' She smiled and went silent, as though waiting for something more from me. Instead, I took a swig from my water bottle. 'It was good to see you out for drinks with us all last week. I know we didn't get to talk much.' *Much?* I swigged again. 'I'm sorry for having startled you when I came to say goodbye.'

'Oh, you didn't...' I trailed off. 'Did I seem startled?'

'You looked quite stressed out when I grabbed you, truthfully.' She laughed. 'Were you expecting someone else?'

'After the last work event I came to, sort of,' I said, trying to sound light.

She shook her head and stood up. 'Pay no mind to that now, M. Things have got to be forgotten eventually.'

By the time I got home I couldn't even bring myself to make dinner. Instead I ordered a personal-sized pizza, slathered with pineapple and onions, and gave the delivery man the door code to let himself into the building. It was a night in for me – and for Caleb. My food arrived as he got home from work. I watched him tug the tie from his neck and loosen his shirt buttons before landing hard on the sofa; he looked like he also needed a personal-sized pizza. But I drew a line at ordering him one. To start with I wouldn't know where to begin with toppings.

I was a slice into my dinner when Caleb disappeared for three minutes and then came back with wet hair and a towel round his waist. His bath towels were brilliant white, which seemed like a brave choice for anyone. They set off the shading in his skin, though, so I had to applaud them for that. He was two steps out of his living room again when he turned back around, as though collared by something, and grabbed his phone. I took another slice and watched him pace the living room, his mobile to his ear. He laughed, shook his head, checked the time, then laughed some more. I ate another slice, suddenly aware of how fast I was chewing, swallowing and reaching for more without thinking. To slow my pace, I stood up and went for a drink, and I brought back a full bottle of non-alcoholic wine to the sofa with me. By then Caleb was out of sight completely.

'Bollocks.'

I took a slice of pizza and the bottle of wine closer to the window.

Caleb reappeared in frame and brought a bundle of clothes with him. He set his phone on the arm of the sofa, as though the call might have ended, but his mouth kept moving. I wondered what sort of a singer he was. But the pauses between what could have been lyrics were too long, and I decided the call was likely ongoing. He struggled into tight-fitting jeans that looked a washed-out blue from this distance. I ate another slice while he forced himself into the fabric. He tugged and shoved and jumped into the legs; Caleb wasn't a big guy but getting into skinny jeans is an unflattering endeavour for anyone. After this he flopped back onto the sofa, exhausted by his efforts. He grabbed the phone and put it to his ear. *There's still time to change your mind then*, I thought, with another mouthful of pizza chased down by fake wine.

It didn't bother me when Caleb made plans without my knowing. But it always threw me off when he had plans that hadn't been planned for. With no trace of a social media event page, it left me blindsided. He spoke for another minute or so by which time I needed to back-step to get more pizza, but I was glued to the view. The last time I'd looked away I'd missed something important and now look at the situation! I chugged wine instead, straight from the bottle as he threw the phone down on the seat next to him and grabbed the chequerboard shirt that he'd brought in. He didn't button and unbutton or double-check his appearance. Instead he grabbed his phone, wallet, keys, everything that had only forty minutes ago been discarded and he made for the door.

It took me thirty minutes to convince myself not to follow him.

SURPRISE

The older you get the worse surprises become.

Caleb's surprise night out ended in me sitting in my living room until two in the morning with the light off. The thought of my silhouette looming large for any onlookers to see shamed me into darkness. But I wanted to know when – if – he'd got home, so I waited it out, despite eventually running out of both pizza and fake wine. He eventually fell through the front door and into his living area, stripping away items of clothing as he went. His jeans were wedged around his knees and I imagined he'd need a good paint stripper to get them the rest of the way off. The shirt he unbuttoned part way down before giving in entirely and pulling the thing over his head, discarding it somewhere on the floor behind him. The boxers were next and I turned away to afford him some modesty. I counted out sixty seconds and then looked back, only to discover the boxers had only made it as far as the jeans, and there'd been no further progress with either. He landed with what I imagined was a thud on the sofa, as though admitting defeat. I went to bed wondering what it is I see in him.

The thought stayed with me until the following day. It had

been a long one at work and the thought of getting home to see him is what carried me through. He was having a night in (although he had plans to be out the morning after), and from his sluggish movements about the place it looked as though he needed to recover.

It was during my habitual scroll of Caleb's social media channels that an announcement popped up in my bottom-right corner: '*Teddy (Theodore) Regis is engaged to Carol Hadlee*'. I let out a near-laugh; *so, parents are of the Facebook official generation.* I hopped over to the post to give it a 'like' and read through the congratulatory comments while I was there. And I wondered what shade of grey the lie I told Mum would be, the next time she asked after Dad.

The thudding was akin to a hangover; the vicious and angry type I could remember from the days when I drank. It took too long for me to realise the banging wasn't internal though. I threw myself from bed, not even checking the time, and paced from the room to find the source. I walked past the front door in time for another thud to land. I'd never been the type to invite angry company, so I peered through the spyhole to see whether I recognised the culprit and there she was: my own mother.

'What on earth are you doing?' I asked in synchronicity with opening the door.

'What on earth are you doing?' she asked back, elbowing her way into the hall. I couldn't account for her response; I was fairly sure it didn't make sense. 'How dare you keep something like this from me?' she continued, slamming open and closed cupboard doors in the kitchen already. When she found a fresh tin of coffee, she finally stopped the banging.

'Please, make yourself at home.' I leaned against the work surface opposite her. 'I'll take one of those. Strong, black.'

She threw a glare at me that I hadn't seen since childhood. 'You'll have what you're given,' she replied, which also felt like something I recognised from my youth.

'Okay, Mum, I'm going to need for you to tell me what's happened.'

She turned, leaving the kettle to boil. 'Were you going to tell me, or was he?'

'He who?'

There was a camera roll of panic where I imagined my mother having watched all my watching. The adult in me soon realised that couldn't be the case; but the child who was being reprimanded by their parent was edgy.

'Your bloody father, who else!' She went back to making coffee. 'There's no use in playing ignorant.'

'You know about the engagement.'

'Yes, loyal and honest child of mine, I bloody do.'

'So, why aren't you banging on *his* door?'

She handed me a mug and walked out, carrying her own. 'Because it wouldn't be right.'

And this is? It was too early for such discomfort in my own home. I followed Mum and sat opposite her in the living room, while I tried to quiet the swell of stress in my stomach. But something in her tone had rankled me. The coffee was too hot to drink but I took a swill anyway, and washed it around my mouth to feel the sting of it while my mother simmered some more.

'It just would have been nice to have been told, that's all.'

'Okay.' From her expression I could see she needed more, so I felt around for something. 'I've only recently found out myself, Mum. I thought of telling you, but I didn't want to upset you.'

'I raised you better. You can't just not tell people things because they'll be upset.'

There was another stab of irritation somewhere that I tried to ignore. But balancing my divorced parents in a manageable fashion hardly seemed a fair means of judging my overall character.

'They've been together a long time.'

'Well, he and I had been.'

'But you're not now.' I tried to imagine I was talking to a small child, or an idiot…

'You don't have to talk to me like I don't understand!'

I rubbed my eyes. 'Mum, how did you even find out?'

'Facebook.'

'But you're not friends with Dad on…' The realisation unfolded slowly. Her face dropped into something I recognised as shame, and I wondered whether habitual stalking could be inherited from parent to child. 'I see.'

'You don't need to judge me.'

'For Christ's sake, how am I judging you?' Almost without my realising, my voice raised a notch in volume. 'You turn up here at a stupid hour, on a weekend no less, banging on the bloody door, because a man you're no longer even on speaking terms with is engaged. Look at it that way, Mum.' I sat forward on the edge of my seat, and felt my face redden as I spoke. 'No longer even on speaking terms with,' I said again, pausing between each word to underscore their meaning. She looked unnerved.

'You need to calm down.'

'Oh, I am sorry. But after that shitshow routine of banging on my front door, I'm the one who needs to calm down?'

'It would have been nice to have been told is all I'm saying. I was riled up after I saw it.'

'I could tell that much.'

'I'm sorry,' she muttered so I hardly heard it. Mum gave me a guarded look, as though wanting to gauge my mood, but also not wanting to look at me. 'I'm sorry if I overreacted,' she added and I noted the 'if', but she looked too unsettled for me to latch onto it. 'He's very important to me, your Dad. We share you, after all, and you're very important to me as well.'

I sighed. 'I know he's important to you, Mum, but he's moved on.'

She took a long hard look at me before she answered. 'You're so much like him,' she said, her tone steady and entirely unreadable. I didn't know whether it was intended as a compliment, or a slap in the face.

THERAPIST

Spilling your innards to a paid stranger is the easiest, guilt-free purge.

When my dad asked whether I'm still seeing my person, he meant Isaac, a counsellor who I started to see some years back. The general practitioners at my doctors' surgery were happy to dump me into the medicated generation. I'd been looking for a quick fix so I agreed. Sertraline helped me to sleep – as long as I remembered to take it first thing in the morning – and it helped me to calm my shit eventually. To begin with the side effects were worse than the symptoms themselves but my prescribing doctor was adamant that that was normal. Once the medication had settled – taking with it the upset stomachs, nausea and brief paranoia – I started to feel like it was making a real difference. There were fewer panic attacks at least, which had been the main thing the doctor wanted to try to treat. He hadn't been too concerned about the other symptoms – which he perhaps should have been. It was those other symptoms that eventually brought me to Isaac; a specialist, and a kind human.

I found it easier to talk to a man than I did a woman – or women, generally. Whenever he asked questions, I felt like brief and blunt answers were enough. He pulled all sorts out of me eventually anyway, without me even trying.

There had been few changes in his office in the time I'd been seeing him; I was grateful for that. It did mean the new plant perched in the corner of the space stood out, though, as did the new photo frame sitting on his desk. I was about to peer over when the door opened and Isaac stepped back into the room.

'Shall we?' He gestured to the comfortable chairs at the far end of the space. He'd always been big on comfort. I guessed that it was a way of tapping into vulnerabilities. 'We may as well get ourselves settled before we chat.'

Isaac was an attractive man. He smiled as I stood up from his visitor's chair and crossed the room, and I imagined he might be watching me while I wasn't looking. Because I judge others by my own behaviours, apparently.

'Do you need a drink?' he asked, sitting down opposite me.

I reached into my bag and pulled out a water bottle.

'Always prepared,' he replied.

'Something like that.'

'How have you been?'

'Oh, you know.' I looked around. 'Generally calm, but that'll be the meds.'

'How's work at the moment?'

I sighed. 'Fine. I seem to have made up with Eleanor.'

'Which is a good thing, isn't it? I know tensions at work were something you were concerned about, the last time we talked.'

'It is. But I don't think she's sincere.'

'Why's that?'

'She needs my help with something.'

'Ah, so you feel a little used?'

I half-laughed. *If only*, I thought. I couldn't remember the last time I'd felt used. 'Not exactly. It's my job, to be helping her with what I'm doing. So, she isn't taking liberties with what she's asking of me.'

'You'd like her interest in you to be about you, not just about work?'

'I think it would help me to be more involved with the place.'

'But you said last time you'd actively withdrawn from things?'

'Only because of the incident with Eleanor.'

'Which you still haven't remembered?'

'No.'

He glanced at his lap where my notes were lying. 'Have you tried to remember?' I don't know what expression I flashed but Isaac let out a low whistle and smiled. 'Okay, we're not there yet. Let's try something else. How are your family?'

'Christ, how are they. Dad's engaged.' Isaac's eyes widened, and I wondered whether Mum's reaction had been more understandable than I'd given her credit for. 'Yeah. Engaged to Carol, who is, you know, fine as a person. Mum promptly flipped a table over it all.'

'Did they argue?'

'No, Mum and I did.'

He frowned. 'Why's that?'

'She pounded down my door to ask why I hadn't told her.'

'Was it your job to tell her?'

'I don't think so, no.'

'Did you communicate that to her?'

I tried to remember, but in the days since the discussion it felt like I'd misplaced parts of it. 'I think so,' I guessed. 'I didn't want to upset her with it all.'

'It wasn't really your place to tell her either, so try to remember that. Are her and your dad any more in touch these days?' I shook my head. 'In that case, it's not only not your job to tell her, but likely it isn't her business to know. They're separate people with separate lives. Whether your dad tells her or not is entirely up to him, and it's not your job to deliver someone else's bad news.' He laughed. 'Bad news which is actually good news. How do you feel about the engagement?'

'Surprised, I suppose.'

'Bad surprised?'

'Not really. Carol is fine.'

'That's the second time you've said that. Have you spent much time with Carol?'

'Not really. She tends to push me and Dad together.'

'In what way?'

'In that, whenever we're having food, I always say to invite her and she never comes.'

'Does she have good reasons for not coming? Other things planned, I mean?'

'I don't know. She sends her apologies through Dad.'

'I see.' Isaac noted something down; I hated it when he did that. 'Is it at all possible that it's your dad who wants the two of you to have time together, rather than Carol?'

'So he's lying to me?'

'For a good reason.'

I wondered what shade of grey that lie would be. 'It's completely possible.'

'Have you thought about reaching out to Carol directly? Now might be a good time for it, to congratulate them both, maybe.'

'I could. I'm friends with her on social media.'

'How are you finding social media at the minute?'

I walked into that one. I dropped my head back, letting my crown lean against the wall behind me. 'I'm trying to cut back on how much I'm using it at home.' There were times when I would tell Isaac what I thought he wanted to hear – which seemed a strange thing to be paying for. But there were times when the truth would fall very much under the 'a danger to themselves or others' catchment, and I wasn't going to go strolling into that so willingly. 'I allow myself an hour or so, just to scope things out.' That was a deep shade of grey, I decided, iron or maybe even shadow.

'Do you think it's helped your stress levels, to reduce the time you're spending on it?'

I laughed. 'Doesn't it reduce everyone's to step away from social media?'

'I don't know that I use it enough to find it stressful.' He smiled and made another note. 'When you were here last time we had a lot of talk about work. Is that a difficult topic this time around?'

'Not especially.'

'But you don't want to talk about the Eleanor incident?' he pushed.

I narrowed my eyes to inspect the suggestion. 'What is there to talk about?'

'Did you try the recall exercises I recommended, for what happened with Eleanor?'

'No, I didn't,' I lied. That was a dark shade too. I had tried the exercise but it hadn't worked, and admitting defeat or failure to Isaac was too much like admitting it to a friend – which I also wouldn't do.

'Are there some things that we could look to try before the next session?'

I couldn't hold back an eye-roll. 'They're difficult.'

'I appreciate that. But they are something we're working towards, and have been working towards for some time. We can agree on that, yes?' I gave a reluctant nod and he continued, 'It doesn't have to be what happened with Eleanor, if that seems like too much of a push. But you should try it for something. Maybe something more recent?'

'I'm sure there's something.'

'So, we can mark that down between this appointment and the next?'

How I loved homework. 'Okay.'

Isaac made a note – presumably of our agreement – and then looked back up at me. He took a deep breath before asking, 'And how have the blackouts been, generally?'

It seemed an unfair question. I mean, really, how could I possibly know?

PART II

ME

I'm an honest person at heart. But also a people-pleaser – and the two don't mix.

My parents, in their own way, noticed that I was a one-size-fits-all when it came to lying for them when I was younger. This was mostly because whatever either of them asked me to corroborate, I would. Whether that was how much money Mum had spent on skirts, shoes and handbags; or whether it was why Dad was late home (although in my defence I never knew the reason for certain myself, I only ever strongly suspected). I have a half-memory of him coming home and emptying the contents of his front pocket into a drawer in his office. He didn't know I was watching.

'Are you hiding sweets, Dad?'

He jumped. 'Christ, kid, you could have warned me you were about.' He took extra care wedging the items as far back as he could before shutting the drawer again. 'Not sweets, no. Something I don't want Mum knowing about, though, deal?' He held up a pinky finger.

I reciprocated the gesture. 'Deal.'

Condoms, it turned out. Loose from a pack, multi-flavoured condoms.

'Has Dad been acting strange around you?' Mum had asked, days later.

'Strange?'

'Strange, like, not himself.'

'Not himself?'

'Jesus.' She turned to face me. 'Is there an echo in here or something?'

I batted between pleasing one and being honest with the other. Pleasing; honest; pleasing; honest... I looked Mum square in the face and said, 'Echo?'

We both fell over ourselves laughing and the original question slipped her mind. Besides, her own time would come when she'd need for me to keep my mouth shut. She eventually found out about the condoms – because my lies aren't that reliable – and rather than approach Dad and have it out with him, she had it out with his credit cards instead – all of them. She maxed out every account she could lay a hand to, including the one that was linked to his business – meaning his partners could see the many (many) purchases made to a reputable sex toy retailer. Years later and Mum hasn't owned up to that part of the payback, instead opting to insist it must have been Dad, even though she and I both know otherwise. People-pleasing won out then; I've never been the slightest bit tempted to tell him the truth.

That said, if either of them were to rest anything too heavy on my young shoulders – heavier than casual infidelities and irresponsible expenditure, that is – I didn't carry the burden well. But not carrying the burden well began to look like not carrying the burden at all in my mid-teens, when I started to misplace things. My parents thought I was being obstinate – to their advantage – to begin with. After some time had passed, they thought I truly was damaged by their years of point-scoring and back-stabbing, even though only so much of it had been retained. Still, it was in their favour.

'Remember, we're not breathing a word of this to your Mum/Dad,' one/both of them would say, and when I made the promise not to, it was because I didn't have anything much to share. It at least allowed me to please people and stay honest – in some ways. So bad behaviour became the proverbial tree in the forest; if you didn't remember doing something, did you really do it at all?

WORK

People love you most when they need you.

I'd started to get uncomfortable around Wendy, mostly because of how comfortable she was getting around me. She was an attractive woman: long legs, blonde hair, a penchant for wearing bright-red clothing which suited her obscenely well. But she also wasn't my type. So when she emailed me for an early morning meeting, complete with coffee and croissants, it felt as though I'd been tricked into having a breakfast date with someone I didn't especially like. She had a sofa in her office and two armchairs, with a squat coffee table centred between them; this is where the pastries and caffeine were. Wendy leaned forward to pour herself a drink.

'Coffee?'

'Please,' I said, not taking my eyes off my laptop screen. We were sitting on the sofa together so she could go through my spreadsheet of publication plans. Or so she could easily rub her bare thigh against my own; that may also have been her motivation. I took the drink from her and swallowed half the cup in two mouthfuls.

'Rough morning?'

I laughed. 'Surely it's too early in the day to be rough?'

'I don't know about that. I had a meeting with the dragon herself first thing.' When I didn't reply, she clarified, 'Eleanor. You know, your best friend.' She nudged me.

'I think Eleanor and I are on better terms at the minute.'

'Because you're the best social media manager we've got, and she's got a campaign.'

'And here I thought she liked me for my mind.'

'Hmm.' She leaned back. 'It does seem to be a good mind.'

I clicked into the sheet for Wendy's earliest release. 'Brockwell?'

'He's a nice chap, he deserves for this book to go well.'

'Well I've got everything staggered over the weeks leading up to publication.' I pointed to indicate the timeline. 'This is when cover releases and snippets from the book are due, and they'll go out at the same time across all our platforms. I've spoken to Keith and he's said he'll be updating the website with the same promos that I've put together for this too.'

'Where are the bloggers factored into this?'

I highlighted a cluster of spreadsheet cells written in red. 'These are the releases for pre-publication, so anyone who has advanced readers' copies to get through. I've got all their social media handles in a separate document, but it's also part of the ARC deal that they tag us in their reviews when they're shared. They'll post them to the usual book sites, too, although that's less my department.'

'Have you eaten?' she asked, in the split second where I was foolish enough to pause for breath.

'I'm not much of a breakfast person.'

'M, come on, I can't eat all of these pastries on my own. Think of my waist.'

Come on, Wendy, you're better than that. Despite being lured into paying her a compliment, I shook away the offer of a croissant. 'Think of my waist,' I said, holding a hand up in protest. If she'd ordered that many pastries to feed one person then shame on her. The more likely explanation was that she had writers coming in throughout the day, and writers – or, starving artists – were a hungry bunch, especially when meeting with an agent.

'Your waist looks fine to me,' she said, relaxing more against me.

'Well it won't do if I eat those pastries,' I replied, trying to sound jovial. *Surely this is sexual harassment?* I thought, scrolling along to the right point in the Brockwell timeline. 'Now, this is where the social media comes in after release day. We have graphics scheduled for release here, here, and here. Brockwell is also doing a social media takeover the evening of his publication day, where he'll be engaging with readers and answering questions.'

'You've dealt with him directly?'

'He emailed me about doing something like this. He didn't mention it?'

She thought. 'No, sly thing, he didn't.'

'Is it a problem?'

'Oh, Wendy just hates it when her authors take initiative and cut her out of something.' Eleanor peered around the corner of the door. I wondered how long she'd been eavesdropping on our breakfast date. 'It makes her feel useless, doesn't it, Wendy? Like you're not even needed.' She smiled; a theatrical and forced expression that perfectly suited her tone.

'We're in a meeting,' Wendy answered, and, despite my disinterest in her as a mate, I had to admit there was something attractive about her dignity.

'I need M for a minute.'

I went to stand up and Wendy set a hand on my arm. 'As I said, we're in a meeting.'

There was a strange moment between the two of them then. One glared at the other with such vengeance. I started to wonder whether this was a preamble for the style of female violence that you only ordinarily find on the Discovery Channel. Trapped between the scorned brunette and the territorial blonde, how will the antelope find a safe way back to their own tribe of computer warriors on the other side of the building?

'M,' Eleanor eventually said, 'are you free this afternoon?'

'I have some time at around three.'

'My office?'

'Is this about the Patis publication?'

Eleanor glanced at Wendy before she answered. 'No, it's about something else.'

I considered asking for the specifics, but the thought of dragging this skewed exchange out longer was an unpleasant one – especially with only half a cup of coffee in me. 'I'll just bring my laptop then and see you at around three.'

'Great.' She looked at the other woman. 'Wendy, pleasure as always.'

'Likewise.' No sooner had Eleanor rounded the corner and Wendy added, 'Bitch.' I was aware of my eyes widening; I couldn't stop the reaction. 'Sorry, M, you shouldn't be caught up in that.' She leaned forward to pick up her mug. 'But you also shouldn't jump to her demands either.'

'Like I said, Eleanor and I are just about back on good terms–'

'Because she needs something.'

I had to admit I felt wounded, even though I knew Wendy was right. 'Still.'

'Still nothing. She can't punish you forever and nothing you said about her was unfair.'

This felt like an opportunity. 'You think so?' I pushed.

'Absolutely. You were well within your rights to say what you did.' She let out a quiet snort of laughter. 'Maybe not within your rights to say it in front of so many people. But, still. Eleanor brings that out in a lot of us.' She sipped her drink. 'Anyway, enough about her, more about Brockwell. Walk me through this publication day thing...'

I was left with the same blank spaces. But I'd seen how people reacted to me, how they looked, and I knew that whatever I'd said wasn't anywhere near as justified as Wendy was trying to convince me it was.

FAMILY

Apologising – whether you're in the wrong or not – is the easiest way to solve an argument.

I was 'making up' to Mum by cooking her dinner, to apologise for an argument I hadn't started or willingly participated in. She'd asked to come over on a Tuesday and I couldn't think of a shareable reason to tell her why Tuesday wouldn't work – or, any Tuesday wouldn't work. Watching the man next door have sofa sex with his non-girlfriend wouldn't have been a legitimate excuse, of that much I was certain, and it felt like a positive thing that I was at least still aware of that. But during my phone call with her I hadn't been able to think fast enough for another reason to come to mind.

'Sure, Tuesday will be fine.'

'Nothing fancy, though, don't go to any trouble.'

She'd already framed this as a 'make up' dinner and, as I was the one who was cooking, I could assume that I was the one making up for something. It wasn't worth an argument about who had started the argument though. Like it wasn't worth an argument over her definition of 'fancy'. I opted for a chicken, pepper, and pitta tray bake and hoped that would be enough to relieve me of the sins of my mother.

Fashionably late, Mum gave me enough time to watch Tuesday arrive. She looked nice, from what I could see of her; tight jeans and a loose top to counteract the heatwave we were having. Her hair was tied up in a messy bun, the likes of which you only ever see donned by beautiful women on Instagram; which is exactly the type of woman she was. She brought in two pizza boxes, which was a change to her normal order, and I wondered whether they were having a pizza each, or sharing two different types – or even whether they'd ordered a pizza accompaniment that happened to come in a similar box. I hated the change; or rather, I hated knowing I wouldn't get to see what the change was. Caleb took the boxes and set them on the sofa before wrapping his arms around Tuesday. He spun her around the living room, squeezed her backside and then set her down again, before disappearing out of sight. *He'll come back with drinks*, I thought, tucking my legs underneath me on the sofa. I would ordinarily be eating with them but–

Mum rang the doorbell (instead of pounding it down with a fist) so I dragged myself away from my viewing. I considered closing the curtains to try to avoid losing focus throughout the evening. But the heat of the room encouraged me to keep them open – at least, that's the excuse I would use.

'Mum,' I stepped aside to let her in, 'come in, get comfy, all the usual business.'

'Thanks, love.' She kissed my cheek. I noticed that she was lugging along with her a large shopping bag, and from the effort it took to move it, it must have been some weight.

'Are you staying for the night?' I laughed, but it was no joke. I'd miss everything.

'No, no, I've been having a clear-out. You know how stuff piles up.' She walked down the hallway as she spoke, seeing herself to the kitchen. 'I found a lot of old stuff of yours that you never did anything with. You might want to chuck the lot,' she diverted to the living room and parked the bag in the corner, 'but there might be things in there you'd like to remember.'

I doubt it. 'Thanks, Mum. Do you want to sit in here for a bit? Much cooler by the open windows than it is anywhere else. We could even eat in here if you like?' I tried to keep my tone level.

'Like when you were little, and we'd have dinner in front of the television?' She smiled at the memory. 'I think it's nice to sit at the table though. Is there anything you need me to do?'

'No, I just need to throw stuff in the oven. Just stay here, enjoy the view.' *One of us should*, I thought, as I paced to the kitchen. The unbearably hot kitchen, thanks to the oven that had been humming away in anticipation of Mum's arrival. 'Do you want a drink?' I shouted as I slid the tray bake in to cook.

'Still no alcohol in the house?'

I sighed. 'No, Mum.'

'Splash of orange juice for me then.'

By the time I took the drinks in Tuesday was topless. They'd skipped pizza and I hadn't even seen it. Or they'd eaten pizza the fastest anyone has ever eaten pizza, and I hadn't seen that. I stood by the windowsill; my face pressed close to the open pane.

'Don't mind me, I just need to cool down.'

'Maybe we should eat in here, if the rest of the place is that hot.'

I watched Tuesday lean back while Caleb kissed her abdomen. 'That's fine with me.'

They ate cold pizza when they'd finished. Like a schoolchild I shifted uncomfortably in front of my accompanying adult, while the feeling in my crotch went from pleasant to embarrassing.

'You're a good little cook, you know,' Mum said, shoving one final piece of chicken into her mouth. 'This has been lovely, just the right thing for this heat.'

'There's some left if you want to take a portion home?'

'Oh, is that my cue to leave?'

Yes. 'No, Mum.' I half-laughed. 'It's your cue to help me eat that tray bake.'

'As long as you're sure.'

There were times AD – After Dad, that is – when cooking was such an effort for Mum that I took over as food-provider. There were times, still, when I reverted. 'More than sure, really. I'll take a portion to work tomorrow as well.'

'How's work going?'

'Oh, you know.' I looked out of the window as though I was thinking. 'It's fine, mostly.'

'You're getting along better with that woman?'

'Getting along a little too well with one of the women, actually,' I said, jovially, and when Mum's eyes widened I laughed. 'She's not really my type.'

'What about the person you're already seeing?' She ran a finger around the edge of the plate and licked at the remains.

'We're not exclusive, really. There are other people on the cards.'

'For the both of you?'

'Mum...' I groaned.

'Oh, so sue me! I care about my child's well-being.'

'Love life isn't well-being.' I stood up and took her plate. 'Now it's your cue to leave.'

She walked with me to the kitchen and leaned against the side while I portioned out my offerings. I gave her the bigger Tupperware box; she needed it more than me, I reasoned.

'You're a love,' she said, taking the food. 'You're sure–' I cut her off with a glance. 'Okay, you're sure.' She kissed my cheek again and headed toward the front door. 'Look after yourself for me, won't you?'

'Always.'

'Love you,' she said, adding another kiss before opening the door. 'Call me, remember to eat and sleep. Oh, and don't forget those memories I left in the living room either.'

I waved goodbye and closed the door, all the while thinking, *how could I possibly?*

HIM

People can surprise and disappoint you in the best and worst ways.

I was sorely disappointed to have missed Caleb and Tuesday; and in many ways I was disappointed in myself for that. I shouldn't have been watching them. But having the option removed left me with a stone in my stomach for the days afterwards. I actively avoided Wendy – and every other authority figure – at work, which included 'not seeing' an email from Gladis Swan herself. She was only asking for social media materials to be brought to the next staff meeting, so in many ways it didn't warrant a reply. I ignored phone calls from both parents too. Mum I knew would be calling for no reason at all, and her rambling voicemail confirmed as much. Dad I was more suspicious of, which gave me even more reason not to answer. He didn't leave a voicemail, which meant it couldn't have been that important (surely). In short, I cocooned, but I rationalised that a nice dinner in front of my windowsill would remedy it all. Despite my new-found unease at these nightly observations of a neighbour.

The heatwave was ongoing and outrageous. Cooking

something felt like a nightmare so instead I made the adult decision to have ice cream as a pre-dinner food. I'd worry about actual dinner when the air was cool enough to breathe easily again. I stripped off from work attire and replaced it with something that actually felt comfortable: shorts and a T-shirt both of which were two sizes too big, and therefore breathable. I'd considered wearing nothing; flouncing about the flat bare, brazen and able to catch my breath. But I knew better than anyone what you could see through these windows.

Caleb always got home from work thirty minutes after I did; sometimes an hour, if it had been a long day for him. But I'd indulged in checking his Twitter – a slip, these things happen – where he'd posted: '*Phew. What a heatwave! Early finish at the office boys. No AC no go.*' So I knew he'd be walking through his front door any minute now.

I ate ice cream straight from the tub while I waited for a sign of life across the street. I was two mouthfuls into my rocky road when he walked backwards into the living room, leading someone in with him. She was a leggy redhead in a floaty dress; perfect for this weather, I imagined. It was covered in a print, either huge polka dots or small butterflies; some things were hard to tell from a distance. Whatever the design, it made her look more innocent than I suspected she was. I recognised these moves of Caleb's; I knew what she was there for. She was average, as far as attractiveness goes; petite around the middle with a nice enough smile. But she certainly wasn't Tuesday.

My hand hovered midway between my mouth and the tub, with ice cream dripping off the edges of my spoon. I couldn't not look but looking didn't feel right somehow; as though I were also being disloyal to Tuesday. Although that thought obviously didn't plague Caleb, as he kissed this woman square on the mouth and grabbed her backside like he had done to his other conquest. Of course, it made sense that someone as attractive as him would have more than one person on the go at any given time. But having gone this long without seeing evidence of it, I'd sort of convinced myself Caleb was above it all. Until, that is, I saw him below her, looking up from a kneeling position.

He lifted her dress, so the hem rested against the base of her stomach, and then kissed her thighs, pausing just before he got – there. I saw her giggle in a way that reminded me of Tuesday and I wondered whether that's why he'd picked her. She rested her hand on his head, tousled his hair, and said something that made him stand upright. They kissed and fondled and touched, and she giggled while he whispered and–

There was a swirl of something in my stomach; something of the bad variety. The longer I watched the more my stress levels stirred, and no amount of good entertainment was worth an anxiety attack. I set my ice cream on the window ledge, spoon and all, and went to my workbag to get my medication. It had been days – maybe longer – since I'd last taken an extra tablet and this felt like the perfect occasion for one. By the time I'd swallowed the pill with a swig of orange juice straight from the carton, they'd disappeared from the window.

My ice cream had left a wet ring on the window ledge that was slowly spreading outwards. The contents were already softening, though, which made it easier to spoon and drink the remainder of the whole thing. I swallowed mouthful and chug after mouthful and chug until the tub was emptied. I felt utterly sick at the end of it – which, I thought, was how I probably should feel about having seen Caleb with someone else.

MEMORIES

Memory lane is an avenue of petty and violent crimes.

The shopping bag of childhood souvenirs Mum brought over lay untouched for most of that week. After the incident with Caleb it took a lot of persuasion for me to get much done; including attending the Friday staff meeting, which I'm sure I did, with little to no memory of what had happened. But Gladis' email – *'Thanks for your notes today. Good to know where you're at with things. Great work.'* – at least saved me the time of worrying about that. It was the following week, when I saw Caleb back with Tuesday that really set me thinking about how things should have been. When she left his flat that night I resolved to tackle the memories that Mum had brought over the week before, with a renewed belief in the idea of things just working out, if you only left them be for long enough. It felt as though my favourite characters on my favourite soap opera had finally made amends.

I began pulling the items out one by one and inspecting them slowly: a Rubik's cube; a picture of a beach I didn't recognise; the ponytail from when I grew my hair out for twelve months, only to decide it was a terrible idea before I cut the whole thing off without warning. They were fond memories, sure, but keeping a huge lock of hair lying around – even if it was my own – wasn't especially appealing.

Despite what Mum thought, I was unlikely to keep much if anything of what she'd brought over. To speed up the process of throwing out my childhood, I upended the bag onto the living-room floor. It vomited out more trinkets – a disposable camera; a GCSE Maths textbook; a scrapbook – and wedged at the bottom there was a shoebox. The bag was such a tight squeeze around the box that I wondered whether I'd have to cut one item or break the other. Leaving that to one side, though, I started with the scrapbook. Graffitied on the front, in a splay of letters that had been ripped from newspapers and rearranged, was my initial along with that of my closest friends – none of whom I was in touch with by the time I hit twenty-three, such is the human way.

I pulled apart the pages slowly. The adhesive holding each picture in place had deteriorated in the years of being unloved, and it was obvious the item needed to be handled with care. There were some photographs that were loose, unsticking entirely as I flicked through memories of me and friends: outside the cinema; on the football field at school; even at the beach that I couldn't recognise from the earlier photograph. *Maybe that came from here?* I wondered, feeling around for the beach photograph, which I wedged into the back of the scrap collection.

Alison and I looked like a cute couple four pages in. Someone had taken a picture of us cuddled up outside school, our faces squeezed tight in the delight of our recent exam results. She'd asked to be a friend on Facebook some years back and I'd politely left the request unacknowledged; deleting it had felt too harsh. Two pages on from this first image there was a similar one, only this time I was making a fake couple with

David. We'd grown closer over the course of our A-Level studies and this image showed us on AS Results Day, our faces beaming with the buzz of a couple of Bs and Cs for subjects we thought we'd failed at.

There were more pictures from results days the following year, where David and I were less close, physically. But seeing the picture prompted a half-memory from the night before that, made up of hurried excitement and fumbled apologies – or maybe that should be fumbled excitement and hurried apologies. It had been good for the both of us to experiment like that, using it as a launch pad for our university days. But we'd agreed it was for the best that we didn't stay in touch. These things ruined friendships and neither of us wanted any jealousy. At least that was what we told ourselves, as we buttoned trousers and pulled on T-shirts in the dark of a friend's spare room.

The further I got into the scrapbook the younger I felt. Eventually I was somewhere in my mid-teens, before the pseudo-stress of GCSEs had arrived. There were small groups of us then, collected in huddles for our pictures to be taken, with one friend or another taking it in turns to be behind the camera. A lot of the images were made up of the same old faces; the familiar collective that had once felt like a tribe. But there were some faces that only appeared once or twice – the girlfriends or boyfriends of friends, brought in long enough for an initiation and a picture, only to disappear a week or so later. We were a scathing and judgemental bunch; teenagers so often are.

There was one face, though, that appeared a handful of times; not every picture but certainly not just the one. She looked a similar age to us, and wasn't out of place with the people she was surrounded by. Jennie and Duncan flanked her in one photograph, their arms so intertwined around each other that it was impossible to work out which limb belonged to which body. They seemed comfortable enough. She was dotted around group photographs, an exclamation in among a string of familiar sentences. I could place their names, and yet...

I skimmed back through the book more, recognising other faces as I went. There was Helen, who only attended our school for five months before being expelled, thereby making her the coolest person to ever grace our year group. Oliver, who was the first among us all to 'come out', only to go back in when he met a girl that he liked in the year below. Rachel and Lily, the twins who swapped places to try out each other's boyfriends. Their names came easily, as well as the chapter and verse of embarrassment that came with our shared years. In some images the girl was there, then not; it became a hide and seek of snapshots. But no matter the pictures, I couldn't find her.

HOMEWORK

Homework doesn't finish when you leave school. It just gets a new name.

The reason I was only seeing Isaac every other week is because during the weeks between I had 'homework'. He asked me to do it often, to build up an understanding of the process, as well as a kind of memory stamina. But there's only so long that any one person can spend sitting in front of a Newton's cradle waiting for a full slideshow to appear. The usual outcome was that there was a collage; a montage of misconnected information.

'But it is all connected,' Isaac told me, the first time I complained. 'Part of retracing these memories is patchworking them together. If you could remember them fully already then you wouldn't need the exercise at all.'

I closed the living-room curtains to avoid distractions. It was late in the day; Caleb would be home any minute, and I only needed an excuse not to concentrate.

The Newton's cradle had been a present – a professional present, that is – from Isaac when I first started to see him for the blackouts. That's what we took to calling them, although in truth I don't think either of us fully understood what they were. Similarly, no general practitioner or subject specialist had been able to understand them either. But several (hundred) pictures of my brain revealed nothing that shouldn't be there. There were no pinprick holes where memories might have tumbled through, as though my short- and long-term stores were nothing more than a sophisticated sieve. That's how I came to think of them, though, as spaces that would hold one thing but not another. The daily tablets were enough to stop me from panicking about the blackouts – which was good, apparently – but no amount of medication stopped the things themselves. One GP eventually decided they must be stress-triggered; the only thing that no one had been able to definitively scan for. To her credit, though, it looked like she was right. I misplaced arguments; bad news; poor tests results; once, an entire break-up. There was only one commonality.

'It's stress,' she said, signing off a fresh prescription. 'Let's try to keep you calm.'

Until that point in my life I hadn't realised there was a pill for it.

I straightened my back, placed two palms flat on my stomach, and concentrated on the noise. The tick-tock filled the room louder than any of the clocks. One ball crashed into another and back again, and I imagined the small vibrations along the chain between the start and end point.

'Think of that start and end as your memory,' Isaac coached me. The first time I'd done this it had been under his supervision and it had resulted in a panic attack. So, I hadn't been overjoyed at the prospect of taking the exercise home. 'But you need that panic, because, in remembering the full memory, you're getting back the panic you didn't allow yourself to experience the first time. Do you see?'

I never did answer; I was too busy trying to catch my breath at the time.

'Pick a point,' he said. 'Pick the last point you can remember.'

I pulled my stomach tight with each in-breath and concentrated on the shape my body became as I exhaled; the fluidity of my belly, and the sudden hunch of my shoulders as though I were literally deflating. I thought about the summer when I found out what cider tasted like: the teenage stress of going home drunk; the worry of navigating woods that had been familiar in the day, and in sobriety; the shock of finding a close friend kissing someone she'd told me only that same evening she hated. In – through the belly, up through the lungs and back again – out. I thought of the walk home that was harder somehow in the dark even though I'd done it before, but without the cider. The cider that tasted like poor judgement and dead apples. Friends had followed me – their teenage stress contagious, worried that I would bring the evening crashing down around their bleary heads – they followed me halfway home before I turned to face them and – in through the belly – I faced them – up through the lungs – but there was a woman who I couldn't place – and back again – because she looked like someone I might have known but a grown-up shouldn't have been in this memory. My friends acted like she wasn't–

There was the first beach party and the fire pit and the panic when a blanket caught. The smallest panic, lit by a stray ember, and when I looked up the same woman was there but she shouldn't have been and then everything went–

'Pick a point you can remember. Before the test results? What about then?'

I wasn't quite not-a-teenager. I remember getting the text message that said positive – in through the belly – and I knew I'd only been with him – up through the lungs – and I remember shouting at him, asking, demanding, who and when and why – up through the lungs – and I grabbed something but that woman–

Dad was shouting at me and asking whether I'd told Mum – up through the lungs – but I couldn't remember what he didn't want me to tell her so I was shouting back and asking, begging – up through the lungs – for him to tell me but then behind him there was the same woman – up through the lungs – who I couldn't place but I saw her for longer and there was something about the face that made me – up through the lungs–

I clattered forward, my palms landed flat on the floor and I was back in the moment – the real one, rather than the remembered. The cradle ticked in the background and I tried to match my body to it; a breath for every two clicks. But there was a pressure in my chest that I recognised as pre-panic.

'Follow your breathing through your body,' Isaac always said. 'Inhale slowly, and imagine the air being pulled in, and swallowed. Imagine where it might move to next...'

After a thirsty inhale, I tried to follow his guidelines. I imagined a small gust travelling through my mouth, down my throat, towards my lungs and into my chest. But the gust re-inflated into a small storm, causing a ruckus as I walked back through the memories that I'd half-recognised – and the woman's face, that I couldn't recognise at all.

CAROL

There are some things we can only do without permission.

In the days after the meditation I couldn't place the woman although I kept seeing her. Not in person, but an imagined version of her; or a memory of the memory of her, which felt like something Isaac would have a field day with. Not through lack of trying, I even repeated the cradle exercise until I nearly had what felt like a full memory of the first bittersweet taste of cheap cider; minus the woman, minus the montage of misconnections. Despite what Isaac thought he knew about meditative memory recall, in the months of trying, it only ever left me with a feeling of diagnosis: fucked.

Later in the week, Dad had called to arrange for dinner and catch-up. After the engagement news, I assumed this one was to announce a pregnancy – twins even.

'Do you want to invite Carol?' I asked.

He hesitated. 'I think it's best we don't, kid. You know what she's like.'

'No, Dad, I don't, but I probably should if you're marrying her.'

'Maybe next time, eh? She likes us to have our time.'

It was only too obvious that I was pissing into the proverbial wind, so I let the issue drop and disconnected the call. I promised to call back when I had my diary in front of me; a definite grey lie given that my diary was in front of me. And I wasn't going to call. But I did take a strategic look through Carol's Facebook page instead. Like most people her age, she posted far too regularly about nothing useful at all. I couldn't stage a run-in with her so I instead did the only other logical thing I could think of: *'Hi Carol. Congratulations (on taking my Dad off my hands haha). I just wondered if you fancied a coffee sometime? Just us! Be good to hang out xx'*. It took her four minutes to reply with a list of days when she was free. We decided on midday Saturday.

I gave Carol the address of my usual coffee shop, and I arrived forty minutes before her. I wasn't scoping the place out so much as I was scoping out the clientele; it had been weeks since I'd been there with Mum. But in remembering that I felt an uneasy shift somewhere; bringing my new Mum for coffee where I took my old Mum. I didn't feel adding, 'So I can see what I've missed,' would help the scenario. Then Dad, Daughter and Mother (who I'd never seen before) walked in and my worries slipped out the door while I was distracted. The three of them wore expressions so sour that I feared for the milk in the place.

'Are you having your usual?' Dad asked.

'Yeah, Mum will like that too.'

'Okay, sit down then, both of you.'

I loved family time.

'Are things okay with you and Dad?' Daughter asked.

The door over obe bell chimed to announce a new arrival and I watched Tired walk in. Ms Tired wasn't behind him, but the Younger Woman I'd seen them with trailed in instead. She caught up with him to catch his hand and he turned; where I'd expected to see outrage there was a smile, and he kissed her cheek. Meanwhile I held on tight to the edges of the table and tried to breathe through the beginnings of an eye twitch. *They're not even embarrassed about what they're doing*, I thought, watching as Tired fondled her in the queue. Even the Dad looked uncomfortable around them, and I'd previously had him down as someone who might enjoy that sort of thing.

By the time they were ordering their overpriced coffees Carol was coughing in my ear to catch my attention, and I was sincerely grateful for the distraction.

'Carol, I'm so sorry, I didn't even spot you,' I said, and stood to hug her. 'I was in a world of my own.'

She laughed. 'Quite all right, dear. Do you know them?' She nodded to the counter.

'No, no, I just thought I did.'

'What can I get you?'

I couldn't even remember draining my cup. 'A flat white, please.'

'Anything to eat, dear? Strength up and all that.'

'I'm meeting friends for dinner this evening,' I patted my stomach, 'saving myself.'

I'd forgotten what a mumsy non-Mum Carol was. Despite her and Dad having been together for so long, she and I had never been close – or never had the opportunity to be. But she'd always been kind during an accidental bump-into-them, and that one time during a family dinner with Dad's side. I couldn't remember much, apart from Carol shovelling potatoes onto my plate while the argument played out behind us, nothing more than a backdrop to her.

'I didn't get cake,' she said, as she sat with our drinks. 'Wedding diet.'

'Well, you don't need to diet, Carol,' I lied again. The lies were coming naturally, and I wondered whether it was an effect Carol had. 'What did you go for?'

'Hazelnut latte.'

'Excellent choice.' *Packed with calories but okay.* 'So, congratulations!'

She let out a girlish squeal and flashed her hand at me. It looked like a knee-jerk reaction. 'Isn't it gorgeous?'

'Beautiful, and nothing short of what you deserve. I think it warrants more than a diamond, taking my dad on,' I joked.

'Oh, he's not so bad.' She stared at the ring as she spoke. 'Thinks very highly of you.'

'I should hope so.'

'Oh.' She laughed. 'Of course. It's lovely to get some time together, though, I was so glad you messaged. I don't want to be a wicked stepmother type.' She reached for my hand across the table and I had to fight the urge to pull it away; I couldn't remember when I'd last been touched. 'You're always welcome under our roof, you know that, don't you?'

There was a level of concern in her that made me think she knew something I didn't.

'That's really kind, Carol.' I squeezed. 'Thank you. I'm just glad we're getting time together now. I'm always grateful for the catch-ups I have with Dad, obviously, when we meet up it's nice and all. But you're always–'

'Oh, you don't need to thank me, dear,' she cut me off, which I didn't like. 'He's told me how unwell you've been, and I know it's important for him to be there for you, but for you to have your privacy too.'

'I'm sorry?'

Her face dropped. 'Have I said the wrong thing?'

Unwell? I took a sip of my drink to buy a second. 'What is it that Dad's told you?'

She held her hands up in a defensive gesture. 'Absolutely not the ins and outs, I can assure you of that much. He only told me things have been hard for a while and that he's been helping you to – oh, I don't know what you kids call it. Work through things, I suppose.' There was a long pause where Carol looked concerned, and I imagined I looked confused. 'Was that the wrong thing as well?'

'Honestly, you're so in the right to bring this up.' I tried to make my tone match my content, rather than mirror my confusion. 'I really appreciate you being so considerate towards our time together, Carol, it helps.' Anyone looking at us would think we were mother and daughter, talking through our teeth and smiles; I wondered who might see us like that. 'Is there anything you want to ask about me, and my, you know, problems?'

She looked shocked at the suggestion. 'Oh, dear, not at all. It's not my place.'

'Of course it is, Mum,' I winked, 'or, Mum Two.' She fell over herself with a blush and a restrained giggle. 'Seriously, anything at all.'

'Well,' she started but she looked hesitant; her eyes were everywhere else. 'Look, don't tell me the details, but are you okay today? After last night I mean? I nearly called you first thing to see whether you were still feeling up to today, but I reasoned you would have called. And I hadn't even seen your dad to ask because he was up and off and,' she paused for breath, 'I haven't even had a chance to tell him I'm seeing you today.' She flicked her hand as though batting something away. 'But that's not the question. Are you okay, dear, really?'

'After last night?' I double-checked and Carol nodded. 'I'm fine, Carol, really. It was good to have Dad there,' I lied. 'I really appreciated the company.' She looked pacified by the answer and promptly changed talk to the wedding. Leaving me to wonder where my dad had been the night before. Because he hadn't been with me. Had he?

FRIENDS

Real friends are the ones who listen to you heavy breathe with panic in the middle of the night.

I'd started having dreams about the girl from the scrapbook, but I hadn't been able to find a shorter name for her. The contents of the bag Mum had brought over were still splayed across their own corner in the living room. I'd hoped that by leaving them on show I might trigger something, but all that came was that same stench of cider. She appeared in every dream, though, as part of the gang, always there on the same night when we got drunk together for the first time. Whenever I saw someone speak to her, her name dropped out of listening range as though she'd been redacted. But I could hear her voice – hear her voice saying my name, even – in the seconds before I woke up. That's always when the panic started.

While I was looking through the scrapbook again, Caleb had friends over. They were crowded into his living room, around a fold-out table that he'd pulled from somewhere. It looked like a boys' poker night without a sniff of Tuesday or The Other One in sight, although I knew one might arrive later. For hours the men were crowded around their fire pits of cards, though, with one of them building a literal house of cards on the table during what must have been a break. Caleb made a show of kicking a table leg and the reverberations made the house fall down – which, seven beers in, the rest of the group seemed to find amusing. He slapped the house's contractor on the shoulder and said something, and the two shared a laugh.

I didn't always like Caleb.

For every picture in the scrapbook I said aloud the names of the people captured. They became affirmations as the process went on, with the same usual suspects appearing in picture after picture. I tried to treat it like any other exercise, with the Newton's cradle clicking in the background to remind me to breathe, but the tick was overshadowed by the sound of my phone ringing when I was two-thirds of the way through the book.

I answered without checking the caller. 'Hello?'

'You met with Carol?'

Dad, doing away with the common courtesies since 1990. 'I did, we had a great time.'

'Yes, she mentioned that much.' His tone was hard-edged, as though Carol and I having a nice time were actually a bad thing. But I couldn't blame his nerves. 'Why didn't she tell me she was meeting with you?'

'Ah, that was my fault. I told her I wanted to talk to her about a surprise and I didn't want you knowing.'

'Right, okay then. Well, what was the surprise?'

I half-laughed. 'That I met with Carol.'

'You're being difficult,' he snapped.

'Sorry, Dad, maybe it's because I'm feeling unwell.' I turned another page and scanned the faces; checked on Caleb and his drunkard comrades; there was still no reply. 'Speaking of feeling unwell, I actually don't feel too great so maybe I could call you another time?'

'Look, it isn't how it–'

I disconnected the call and put my phone on silent.

He'd ruined the read-through so I started the scrapbook afresh. I dug around the flat until I found a pen and paper, to start writing down every name as I said it out loud. For some I could find surnames and for others I couldn't; that happens naturally to our memories, I reasoned. It was nothing to do with the girl. But there was a long enough list coming together. By the end of it there were twenty-three names, eighteen of which had surnames too; it was enough information to find them.

When I came up for air – and my laptop – Caleb's group had whittled down to him and another two men. After spending a whole evening looking at photo stills, it was nice to see other humans – animated ones. Something caught the attention of all the men at once, though, and their heads snapped in the direction of the front door. Seconds later, Tuesday appeared, which wasn't at all right for a Sunday evening and I wondered whether Caleb had called her. The best part of the night had gone now, and it didn't take a genius. I stalled, too, at the thought of how she'd even got in. *Does she have a key to his apartment?* No sooner had she arrived, taking a seat at the men's table, and the remaining players upped and left as though she'd given them a cue. They each high-fived Caleb on their exits, and it looked like they said a quick goodbye to Tuesday each as well.

It took me less than a minute to find my laptop and its cable, stashed away in my workbag still. Yet by the time I'd come back Caleb had managed to get Tuesday half undressed and astride him. Since seeing him with The Other One I wondered whether this kind of lunacy was something he brought out in women.

I keyed in my password and powered up my social media feeds, opting for Facebook first. I'd need to show people pictures, I decided, so I used my phone – clearing the five missed calls from Dad scattered through the last three hours –

to take shots of the scrapbook. Each picture I took showed a cluster of familiar faces, and the girl. When I needed to explain myself in the message, scrapbooking seemed like the obvious reason for wanting to remember names. So I drafted something – '*Hey, long time! I'm working on a scrapbook project and the names I've lost over the years...*' – and took care not to send pictures to the wrong people. The message stayed closed in a Word document for later use and I typed in the first full name on my list to see who the lucky recipient would be. The website stirred and sifted through names with an obvious reluctance, leaving me enough time to glance up at them.

They had no shame in what they were doing. Their bodies were framed by the open window and they were, I decided, exhibitionists who didn't care. That, or they were simply so lost in one another...

I crossed the room and closed the curtains. I wasn't in the mood to watch.

RESEARCH

A watched pot is never read – or something to that effect.
I'd taken to checking my Messenger with increasing regularity. But thanks to the Safety and Privacy Gods of Social Media, my research into the misremembered girl meant I had to wait on people to accept my offer of a message, before they could unknowingly accept my inquisition. I'd contacted David, Duncan, Helen and other semi-strangers who I'd been able to find. I'd scoured their friends lists to put surnames to the faces I hadn't been able to place too. But either they weren't as active on social media as I needed them to be – three full days had passed – or they didn't feel like a walk down memory avenue. If it were the latter, I couldn't blame them.

'Who are you waiting on?' Wendy appeared behind me.

'Bloody writers who don't have their details listed online.' The lie came easily; I realised I'd been ready for someone to ask. 'But I can try again tomorrow.' I turned and closed the browser windows behind me, before shutting down my computer.

'Are you heading straight home, or do you have plans?'

I sucked in a greedy amount of air and said, 'Dinner date, actually.'

'Oh.' When I started to pack my bag to leave she added, 'Someone new, or special?'

Wendy took a step backwards as I stood from my desk, my full backpack in hand as a signpost that I really was ready to leave. I forced a laugh. 'Can they be both?'

She smiled. 'I suppose they can.' She took another step back then. 'Well, have fun.'

'Thanks, Wendy, you have a good evening yourself.'

Our conversation lulled naturally and I left, treading down the corridor towards the exit with a heavy gratitude that she hadn't followed me. But there was still a worry of her watching.

It had started to feel like I was losing touch with Caleb. I reasoned that dinner would bring us closer together for an evening at least. On the way home I stopped for the necessary supplies and, once home, I threw everything together to boil while I changed from work to comfort. Caleb arrived home over an hour after me which meant a couple of things. Firstly, I'd had time to rearrange furniture to accommodate dinner. Secondly, he must have had a terrible day. I watched as he loosened his tie and landed heavily on the sofa. There was a tug of sadness in me to see him look so deflated. I'd made too much pasta and, shovelling fusilli into my mouth, I wondered whether a Tupperware dinner on the doorstep would be a line worth crossing. I reasoned that it likely wasn't.

After undressing in the living room, he walked through the office-dining room next door and then out of sight. For a shower, I guessed, after a few minutes – and mouthfuls – had passed. So I brought my laptop to my dining table and loaded his separate profiles. There was nothing of use on Instagram; the last post had been from his evening with the boys, a simple square of chips, cards and beer bottles, captioned: '*Lads and poker. What could go wrong? #needsmust #treatyourself*'. There wasn't a story to watch, and he hadn't been tagged in any pictures either, so I closed the browser and moved on to the next. Twitter was a mess of retweets about sporting news but, even as I scrolled through them, his timeline stuttered as 'One new update' arrived at the top of the screen. There was a warm feeling in me that he was updating it at that very moment. I hit the button to take me straight to the top that read: '*Rough day at the office. But footie and food now. Roll on @steakandbake delivery*'. Steak and Bake was a pie shop in the city centre; their niche being that they weren't in any way gastro.

Caleb walked back into view with his phone in hand. I imagined him closing Twitter at the same time as I did. He was wearing what looked like jogging bottoms – which he only ever put on for home – and a plain yellow T-shirt. So, I knew he wasn't expecting company. We were both comfortable for the evening now.

His Facebook showed much more activity. I read and scrolled and continued to shovel pasta, trying to sift through funny videos and shared awareness posts to get to the real meat of things. He'd been updating his statuses more often but there was no mention of The Redhead – or Tuesday – in any of them. Whenever he checked in somewhere he checked in with friends, most of whom were male. I skimmed the profile pictures of the females mentioned just in case but there was still no sign. There were several places listed where he'd checked in more than once, and usually at the same time each time he went. I grabbed a Post-it note to write them down. There was no pattern to the days he was going, so updating my diary didn't seem worthwhile. But having the places to hand couldn't hurt.

The most recent posts looked to be events he was attending, and encouraging others to attend: a charity fundraiser; a community football match; a classic Ibiza night at a club in town. There was a handful of comments on each but, again, nothing from the women. I wondered whether he kept them away from his social media deliberately; whether Caleb could be so clever, or rather, calculating. I didn't like to think it of him, but still.

He was on the sofa when I left to find my diary. By the time I came back he'd made himself comfortable, his legs splayed, the way they do, while he flicked through television channels. The night wasn't the reconnection I'd hoped it would be, although it was helping. There was some comfort, I thought. But the music was missing! I connected my phone to the speaker, flicked to our playlist. Morrissey filled the room. It wasn't my favourite song, but Caleb had attended more than his share of tribute nights – according to a back catalogue of embarrassing photographs online – so I tried to choose a few tracks that I guessed would be to his taste. I listened and watched while he changed channels in the opposite building still. When the track changed to Blondie he stood up and disappeared in the direction of the front door. He came back with a neat brown paper bag and, animal that Caleb was, he pulled out the contents and spread them across the coffee table without the hassle of a plate.

When Caleb was tired, or without company, he ate like he hadn't seen food in months. I watched him snatch and grab and pinch, at pieces of pie and a side of chips until my stomach couldn't take it any longer. Then I went back to his social media, rifling through comments on posts for upcoming events to see whether Tuesday was a likely companion for him. She had to be there somewhere, I reasoned. Although the thought crossed my mind that she might be in another block of flats somewhere in the city, doing the exact same thing as me.

I was about to click into another event when my screen froze for a second, and then there appeared a chat box in the bottom corner: '*Helen has accepted your request. You can now contact each other*'. Three small dots danced along the bottom of our conversation window. I didn't realise I was holding my breath until it burst out of me in a hurried sigh. *How much can one woman write?* I wondered, as I watched a full minute roll by. But then the reply came, signalled by a happy ping from my speakers: '*Hey! Wow, it really has been a long time. It's so good to hear from you...*'

'Yada, yada.'

I skimmed the message through to the bottom: '*Now, these are some familiar faces. Let's see. I'd say bottom right looks like Lucy Given, next to her there's Jason — can't remember his last name. And god there's a name I really haven't heard for a few years. On the left side, I'd say that's Fern Norton.*'

HER

Everyone loves a sweetheart.

Fern Norton did relatively well at her GCSE exams but got distracted by new friends and new surroundings. No one thought ill of this or judged her for it; although they might have done for any other teenager who was hitting booze every weekend with their friends. Her family moved from London to the outer limits of Birmingham in the summer when Fern turned fifteen. It looked as though this move only happened because her dad, Elliot, got a job working in the city proper. There didn't look to be any animosity between him and Jessica, Fern's mum, who commented freely that the move was a welcome change – especially after so many years spent inside the gutter of London. Elliot was an accountant and Jessica used to be a teacher before she gave up conventional work to be a full-time parent to Fern, her firstborn, and the three siblings who came after. It was difficult to find their names.

Fern joined Newtown Middle School for her second year of GCSE studies and immediately fit in with a large enough friendship circle. She was welcomed among them all and looked to be well-liked, if the quotes and comments were anything to go by. Most people thought of Fern as 'bubbly', 'funny' and 'so, so clever'. The latter, at least, was confirmed by the A-Level choices that she'd signed up for, namely: Maths, Further Maths and Business Studies. There was no mention of Politics as a subject interest until it came to her aspirations for university, but students change their minds a lot during teenage years. Her teachers thought similarly of her to her friends; that Fern was funny, approachable and quick to make friends. Although given that she was a pretty girl in a new school it seemed probable that she was quick to make enemies as well.

And she was a pretty girl. In every picture of her, her hair was a dusty brown with a blonde tint that could be highlights but could also be good old-fashioned luck insofar as her genetics. The few pictures of her parents showed that they were an attractive coupling, so a genetic jackpot for their offspring made sense. Fern only wore mascara, which made her both wide- and bright-eyed in every image, too, her eyes themselves being a dark green. She might have worn foundation; there weren't many spots to be seen and for a girl of her age that seemed unlikely, without some cosmetic assistance. She was only ever pictured from the one side, too, and always with her head tilted at an angle. Fern, like most women, then, had learnt at a young age what her 'good side' was when there was a camera around. But they're just observations; it's nothing concrete.

From all reports it looked as though Fern had a charmed life. Her parents were happy and together; her siblings were a decent enough age apart not to hate each other too much; she had friends at school and a bright future.

Until she died, that is – quite unexpectedly – as teenage girls sometimes do.

Twelve years ago, Fern left a woodland celebration with friends to return home. A group of them had gathered around a campfire, dangerously lit at the edge of Wayfare Woodland Park (it had been closed down since, due to fire damage and unsteady tree structures overhead). It was their GCSE results night and most of the teenagers from Fern's year were out celebrating their achievements. The school had a sixth form college attached to it, so it was a common and largely correct assumption that many of them would be staying together for another two years of study – apart from the ones who didn't make it in, who were drowning their sorrows elsewhere. This celebratory circle each brought an offering: a bottle of low-alcohol wine; two bottles of WKD; one even brought a small bottle of vodka although the person responsible was carted home well before the end of the night. It was a share and share alike situation, where the booze was kept together and as long as someone had brought something then they were free to help themselves to whatever someone else had brought. The parents regretted this, in the end, but it was a harmless offering at the time.

Around the group they'd taken it in turns earlier that day to ask their parents, 'Can I stay at so-and-so's house tonight?' and the parents had mostly agreed – another regret. So, along with the precious alcohol supplies, there were also small amounts of food on offer – pilfered from parents' kitchens – and there were sleeping bags and roll-out mats for those who were opting for a night under the stars. It had sounded romantic at the time, no doubt, but the vomiting and heaving put a stop to the romanticism, and some ended up going home well before planned.

Not everyone left because of early onset alcohol poisoning, though, some people had just had enough. Even though there was a large circle of friends involved, every circle has their cliques. The most popular teenagers, high on bubbles and their first licks of summer loving, started to couple off, leaving the less popular ones to make their own entertainment. The latter, deciding there was better entertainment to be had at home, dissipated, leaving behind an inner circle. But Fern, one of the popular ones who had paired up with Bradley Scott, opted to leave too. She'd told her remaining friends that she'd be right back but that was the last they saw of her. That is, until the police arrived at their houses two days later with a picture of Fern, asking whether they recognised her; whether they could tell them anything about results night.

But I couldn't remember much at the time, other than coming home early – other than a friend coming after me. I think I remember something now though; not much, but something.

PART III

ME

I'm an honest person at heart. But people can only be as honest as others allow them to be.

I can't remember the first time I didn't remember something. But I can remember the first time my parents noticed I didn't remember something. In the hours after mock examination results were revealed, sometime before the weight of GCSEs had really landed on me, I casually told my parents that my grades were failing ones. It was nothing, and I said it like it was nothing, midway through scooping mashed potato into my mouth while we all sat around the dinner table. But Mum froze.

'What do you mean, failing?'

I laughed. 'Failing like, not passing.'

'So, how are you going to get into college?' Dad asked. 'A Levels, remember?'

'I'll worry about that in the next two years.' I set my fork down. 'Come on, they're nothing. Even the teachers told us not to worry about them.'

'Because your teachers won't have to support you once you're kicked out of school,' Mum answered, her tone rising and rippling with panic around the edges.

'How am I suddenly getting kicked out of school?'
'Don't talk to your mother like she's an idiot,' Dad chimed in.
'Well she's act–'
'Don't you dare,' Mum cut me off.

Things were tense the following morning. Mum would usually set out breakfast things galore to give me and Dad options, but there was nothing more than bread and spread available. Dad had already left for work when I got downstairs but Mum was there, sat at the table as though she were waiting for me.

'Is everything okay?' I asked, with my back to her while I pulled a mug from the cupboard. I didn't even wait for a response before adding, 'Do you want a tea?' When she didn't answer I turned around and spotted that she was already holding a mug, cradled between her hands like a small bird. 'Oh, sorry, never mind.'

Mum didn't say a word while I boiled water, added the teabag, dug out the milk; nor while I loaded the toaster with bread. She waited until I was sat across from her, tearing the crusts from my toast.

'I think we need to talk.'

'Okay,' I carried on eating all the while, 'about what?'

She narrowed her eyes at me, as though searching me for something. 'Last night.'

'About my mock exams, you mean?'

'Sort of about that, but also about...' she petered out. 'The way you spoke, last night.'

'I'm genuinely sorry about that, Mum.' I washed my toast down with two mouthfuls of tea. I didn't really have time for a long apology if I wanted to catch my car-share to school. 'I know that I could have found a better way to tell you.'

'It wasn't the telling that was the problem.'

'Then...' I let my question go unfinished.

'You don't see a problem with last night?' she asked, and she looked genuinely confused. Although my expression stayed blank. I shook my head gently and waited for more from her. She eventually sank back in her seat and repeated, 'You don't see a problem with last night.' And it didn't feel like a question anymore.

A car horn sounded from outside and I slugged down the rest of my tea.

'I'm really sorry, Mum, honestly. We can talk more later? Love you.'

Mum didn't need to talk to me later, though, she needed to talk to Dad. I overhead them; that is, I sat at the top of the stairs like a small child and listened.

'I'm telling you, there was no recollection of last night at all.'

'Pssh,' Dad answered. 'You can't know that. It's teenage pranks.'

'It isn't, I'm telling you–'

'You never pretended to forget something to get out of answering for it?'

'I might have done, but I didn't pretend to forget an argument from twelve hours earlier, did you?' Mum snapped, and there was a long silence after that where I imagined Dad thinking carefully about his answer. 'You can brush it off as much as you like but I'm telling you, there was no hint of recollection or remorse there, none. It was like looking at a blank slate.'

'So, what you are saying? Are you saying it's a blackout, is that a thing?'

'I don't know what I'm saying. Jesus, why do you – I don't know what I'm saying,' Mum repeated herself again and I felt sorry that Dad and I were sending her in loops. 'I'm saying that something was missing, that's all I'm saying. That's as much as I know.'

There was a silence then where I thought Dad might have reached across the table to give her hand a squeeze; or I hoped he had. 'I see,' he said. 'I think I see.'

INTERROGATION

When you can't find the answer online, ask someone else. Mum hadn't invited me over to dinner for a while. So it wasn't the most intrusive thing for me to invite myself over one evening. Although it occurred to me half an hour after texting – '*Dinner at yours? X*' – that the only way to counteract the assumed invite would be to at least offer something in return – '*I can even cook if you like x*' – which was an offer that Mum found particularly amusing: '*LOL. Dinner wud b gr8 xx bring pud xx I'll cook*'. Mum was of the generation that had learnt to text using text-speak and would therefore continue to use it forever – no matter how many texts they were afforded on their contracts. I'd tried to get her into the world of WhatsApp but apparently that was a step too far.

We timed it so I could get home from work and get changed, which meant I didn't have to take the detritus of the day out with me. It also meant I could spend a cup of tea – a standardised measurement of time, that is – with Caleb when he came in from work. He walked in alone, which was a relief because the last few weeks had prepared me for anything. I still hadn't been able to find The Redhead on any of his social media; I'd looked through followers and friends as well as commenters. The only way to keep her from it all, I reasoned, would be if she didn't know him at all – if she couldn't find him. I wondered whether Caleb had given her a fake name when they met; who was he to her?

My alarm sounded so I ditched the remains of my cold tea and got changed into something that passed as presentable, although it was secretly comfortable clothing. It only took fifteen minutes to walk through the city and arrive at my mum's which meant that by the time I was buzzing into her building – 'It's me, your favourite child.' – I was early. I'd stopped to collect a cherry pie on the journey over, too, although it was packaged to facilitate a lie.

'Fresh from my home to yours,' I said as I handed it over and Mum eyed it with some suspicion. 'Okay, not my home exactly. But it's the food of my city.'

'We live in the same city.'

'All right, the food of our city.'

'Cherry pie isn't the food of Bir–'

'Okay, fine, whatever, I'm a rubbish guest.' I gave her a squeeze and headed to the kitchen. 'But you didn't specify the pudding had to be home-cooked.'

'Which is fine,' she said as she opened the oven door, 'because you didn't specify that dinner did either.' Mum pulled out a tray packed with silver containers and paper lids, each marked with a number that, I guessed, corresponded to a menu item. 'Am I a rubbish mother for feeding you grease?'

I kissed her on the cheek. 'You're the best, for that very reason.'

'Grab the plates, would you? I put them to heat.' She set the tray down on the kitchen counter and started to take the lids away. 'I had no idea what you wanted, or what I wanted.'

'So you ordered one of everything?'

'No, I ordered…' she petered out. 'Okay, so sue me.'

We both sat down with plates heaving full of food, more than either of us would eat – such was the takeaway tradition. I didn't want the distraction of Fern over dinner, so I asked Mum about the one topic I knew would set her talking: love. She told me about men she'd been talking to online – 'I know how you feel about it, but…' – and I half-listened while I ate rice and noodles and roasted vegetables. There was something in her, excitement, I guessed, that I hadn't seen for a while.

'It's nice to have company.' She threw her napkin down. 'And now, I've told you a boatload you don't really want to know about. What's happening with you?'

'Ah, everything is average. Work is fine, the person I'm seeing is,' I hesitated. 'Fine.'

'Nice try.' She pulled the plate away. 'I'll wash. You wipe and tell me what's up.'

She set water running and turned away to fetch the pie.

'Mum, do you remember Fern Norton?' I asked, and she froze facing away from me.

'Christ, of course I do.' She put the pie in the oven on a low heat. 'Why?'

'There were some pictures of her in the bag you brought over.'

'Oh, I'm sorry, love. I should have – well, I should have thought.'

'No, it's okay,' I said, hunting for a towel. 'I just wondered what you remembered.'

She looked deeply into the running water, and I imagined melancholic music playing behind her when she spoke. 'Honestly, it feels like yesterday. All your friends hounded, poor Fern's parents hounded, it was a horrible time for a lot of people.'

'But do you know what happened to her?'

Mum shot me a look. 'You mean, how she died?'

'The papers didn't say much about it and, seeing the pictures, I just...'

'She was hit over the head with something, by all accounts. Her body was dumped in the bloody woodlands like she was nothing.' I'd read that part online; the woodlands had been a perfect backdrop for the media coverage. 'Those old woods were such a mess, it's no wonder they couldn't work out what was what on her. Whoever did it, they thought about it long and hard. Scumbag.' She shook her head. 'Sorry, love, what – I mean, were you okay, finding her photographs?'

'See, that's the thing. I don't really,' she turned to face me as I spoke, 'remember.'

'What, anything?'

'Everyone loses some of their teenage years, right?' I tried to laugh it off but in my peripherals I could see her raised eyebrows. 'Did the police come to see me?'

'Only the once. You were there, of course.' She said it like it was obvious, so I tried not to react. 'But you'd come home before Fern, you said, and others said. You said she was fine when you'd left, and others said exactly that too.' She nudged me. 'You weren't as much of a boozehound as the others, I don't think.'

I laughed. 'Still not.'

'Big slice or little?' she asked as she pulled the pie out.

'Little. I'm stuffed. Were Fern and I close, Mum?'

'Ah, you weren't especially close. There was a big group of you, though, so some of you were closer than others, you know how it is.' She found a knife and cut through the pastry; there was an audible crunch. 'Oh, lovely stuff this is.'

'And after she died, what were things like then?'

She sighed. 'In the town, you mean, or with you?'

'Both?'

'The town changed, love, of course it did. Places do when

someone dies, especially someone like Fern.' I wondered exactly what she meant; someone young, or someone pretty, or someone female? Did it make it worse, somehow, that she was all three? 'You struggled a lot, but most of your friends did too. First taste of grief, I suppose. The funeral was especially hard. Pass the plates, would you?'

'Why was it hard?' I followed instructions.

'Seeing Fern's family was a lot for you, I think. The kids did it, you know, her brothers and her little sister. You were brave for a lot of it, credit to you, but I think seeing her mum was too much.' She paused. 'Seeing her mum really tipped you over, that day.' There was an abruptness to the way she set the knife down next to her, and the clang made me flinch. 'You don't remember any of this?' she asked, with a suspicion that I recognised.

'It was a long time ago, Mum, and I was a kid,' I said, reaching round her to grab the two plates. *But no*, I thought, *I don't remember these parts at all.*

WORK

Anyone who spends their full workday working is a liar.

Agents and authors alike change their minds about things too often to keep track of. I was ahead with my social media scheduling until Eleanor changed her mind on the Morgan campaign; which meant she also had to change her mind about the Bourne one. The authors were writing in similar genres so pushing one back meant encroaching on another, and the explanation droned on until I said, 'Should you consult the authors on this too?'

'I'm sorry?' Eleanor batted her eyelashes in what I thought was surprise. I opened my mouth to answer but it was clear she didn't need further input. 'I'm sorry, M,' she landed hard on my 'name', 'I didn't realise you were secretly a literary agent. I'll just go right ahead and check all of this over with the authors, like you suggested.'

I watched her walk away; her full hips gave her a gait that belonged to the likes of Jessica Rabbit, so it was understandable how she got away with as much as she did around the office. But the fact that she didn't appear minutes later to revise the campaigns with me in person made me think she was, in fact, checking with the authors.

It left a hole in my schedule. I checked emails, watched colleagues, saw Fred wink at Wendy in a way that she didn't look entirely approving of. It only killed so much time and took up so much headspace; before I knew it, I was thinking of her again. I'd started thinking of her as often as I was thinking of him, although I couldn't spot a connection between the two.

I pulled up Caleb's Twitter page – the one most likely to be updated during the workday – but there was nothing I'd missed. Outside of my allotted time for it, I'd started to check in on him at the same time as I checked in on my work profiles; first thing every morning, and occasionally throughout the day. It was a distractor task to stop me from thinking of her but it didn't always work. With nothing fresh to read from Caleb, I pulled up a search engine and tried to find Fern again. There were hundreds of pictures of her listed under the 'Images' tab at the top of the screen and I wondered where they'd come from. Some would have been released, I guessed, as part of the investigation. But Fern with friends, Fern at school, Fern playing with her siblings in the back garden. Had they been stripped from social media without her consent? It happened to young girls so often these days.

There were headlines fixed to every anniversary since her death, and pictures of flowers that had been left at the boundaries of the woods. By her family, I hoped, but there were always people hungry for death, leaving posies behind like that. The further back I scrolled the more tenuous the reporting became. Although I did find one article lampooning the police investigation for not looking closer at the family: '*It's common knowledge that the family were on the verge of a break-up after moving to a city for the victim's father to take new work*'. Common knowledge seemed a stretch from everything else I'd read, but there were desperate reporters all over the world looking for controversy. I closed the window and marked them down as a clinger-on.

It was on page two of these search results that I found something more useful: *Looking through the ferns: The Fern Norton case*. The title was enough to make anyone heave; although I imagined the author thought highly of themselves for having come up with it. Still, from the brief window description it looked to be the sort of guidebook I needed.

'Not his finest work.' Wendy's voice made me jerk. 'Oh.' She laughed. 'I'm sorry.'

I turned to face her. 'No, no trouble.' I didn't like how I could never see her coming. 'What do you mean, though, sorry?'

She nodded to the screen behind me. 'Danks, he's one of our authors.'

'We published this?'

'Ha, no, we absolutely didn't. It was a labour of love on his part. He lived nearby to where the girl was murdered if memory serves. Apparently it was quite a time. It wasn't too far out of the city, was it?'

I tried to focus on every word; she sounded like she was underwater. 'No, not too far. This Danks, he's a kind of expert on it, then?'

She laughed. 'Aren't authors experts on everything they write about?'

'Well, I suppose they think they are which is basically the same thing.' I tried to keep my tone level. I wondered whether she could hear the thrum in my ribcage or whether it was an inside noise. 'Danks is still under you?'

'I wouldn't put it quite like that.' She winked. 'But he's still working with us. It's more that his, oh, whatever you call it, true crime, local interest, that side is all self-published. He doesn't even run it by me.'

'It sounds like you wouldn't publish it anyway, even if he did.'

'No, I suppose not. We might have considered the Fern publication, though, if he'd let us edit it, shape it up a little better somehow.' She pursed her lips and thought. 'It could have been a good book if he'd been more imaginative with it.'

'Imaginative? I thought true crime was meant to be factual.'

She gave me a soft look, like I was a gullible creature. 'To a degree. There's good money in books about dead girls, though, so it really is a shame.' The thrum leapt into my throat then, and answers slipped by the wayside. 'Don't bother buying a copy, if you decide to read it. Danks sent me a paperback when he published it, so you can borrow mine. It's in my office.'

She didn't wait for a reply before she left. I craned around my monitor and watched as she walked down the corridor. The panic I'd felt started to ease then, too, and I imagined a small string wrapped around it, tied to Wendy's waist; the further she walked, the slower my heartbeat. Although she'd probably take a quickened heartbeat as a compliment.

I took in greedy amounts of air and clicked onto the webpage for the book. The order confirmation screen told me my delivery would arrive in three to five business days.

HIM

Time flies when you stop scratching off the days on your work calendar.

I got home from another exhausting day of avoiding Wendy. It occurred to me that we were getting to the point of needing to discuss matters with Human Resources. But then I realised how unlikely it was, that she was the one harassing me. I'd rolled the idea around, and given up on it, several times over. Opting instead to duck into empty cubicles and follow people to the drinks dispenser to avoid one-to-one conversations. But there was still the matter of her authors, which required meetings – in Wendy's office.

'She's taken a real shine to you,' Fred said while I was filling my coffee cup.

'Wendy?'

'Come on, like you haven't noticed. Don't be dog about it.' He nudged my arm.

'Wendy can do better than me.'

'Hey, don't put yourself down, man, you're a catch.' He leaned heavy on the word 'man' so I knew this was a friendly compliment rather than an attempt at flirting. 'You're not into her, though, right?' I hesitated too long on my answer and he leapt on it. 'Oh, oh, I get it. You're not that way inclined?'

I moved away from the coffee machine. 'I guess she's just not my type, no.'

'To each his own, to each his own,' he said, jabbing buttons.

It had been a long day. But I rested my head back on the wall behind the sofa and tilted my view towards the window – and I watched. For the first time in what felt like days, I concentrated only on my breathing, and on waiting for the change of light in Caleb's living room to show he'd finally come home. *It must be a late finish*, I reasoned. The longer I waited, though, the less I wanted to move for fear that I might miss the coming home altogether; the loosening of the tie and the heavy thud of him landing on the sofa, still in his work clothes. When the sky darkened, I stood up to get my phone, to check on him as best as I could, but then the overhead light snapped on in the living room opposite. Enter Caleb – with Tuesday.

I hadn't even realised the day until I saw them together.

Neither of them were carrying food containers, though, and I wondered whether they'd been out for dinner – whether that might account for the lateness. That would, of course, also mean that Caleb had taken her out into the real live world of eateries and being seen in public. But what about The Redhead?

I watched as their usual routine rolled into Caleb's usual routine. Tuesday started to loosen his tie long before either of them made it to the sofa. Caleb reached his own buttons and it looked like she stopped him. I wondered whether she enjoyed this act of undressing more, the intimacy of having come from work together. It must have been a special moment for them.

I hadn't eaten since lunchtime and the growl from my gut told me that I needed to. But I couldn't tear myself away for fear of missing something more than I'd already missed. The most I managed was to feel through my bag for my mobile phone, and

I thumbed to Caleb's Twitter profile. Stealing glances between reading tweets and watching fabric stripped from skins, I saw that he'd been out for dinner, and with someone: *'Looking forward to a meal out with @louisesoumedia later tonight. Bring on the burgers @classiccarter'*. Caleb had name-dropped so many restaurants in the time I'd known him that I wondered whether he was enrolled in a sponsorship programme with local businesses; he was attractive enough. Louise Sou Media was a new name to me, though, so I clicked into the attached profile – and there she was, Tuesday.

They hadn't even made it to the sofa, instead opting for the closest wall and I looked from profile to real-life image and back again. She looked different without her clothes on, but I supposed most people did. Louise Sou Thackerey was a freelance media consultant who earlier that day tweeted: *'Can't wait to fill my face with @calebcanteachya later tonight! Gimme burgers boy!'* I looked from profile to real-life and back again and wondered whether *'fill my face'* had been a euphemism. Neither of their tweets looked romantic, though, which seemed strange given the displays I'd seen at home.

I watched them for a minute, to check Tuesday was still pinned in place. From their speed it didn't look like they were going anywhere. This was their version of tender, I guessed, from how I'd seen them behave before. And while I tried to be pleased at their advancing relationship, there was something bitter in my stomach – as well as a growing hunger.

Tuesday's tweets had three replies attached, public to view, while Caleb's had none. I carefully clicked for the answers to unfold, mindful not to give her an accidental 'like' while I was at it. One reply was from Caleb – *'Get in my beeeeeelly'* – but another reply – *'Hope you two have the best time babes'* – was from a face I recognised. Tuesday had replied to this one – *'Thanks honey bee. Drinks soon?'* But The Redhead hadn't answered that one.

I clicked out of Twitter and threw my phone back on the sofa. They were nearly finished, and I liked to watch the end. But that safe distance was for the best, I decided. Because for all my watching, there were things about Caleb I was only just starting to see.

FRIENDS

There are times when a little help from your friends is actually what you need.

Mary called and I could hardly hear her. There was the lively bustle in the background that I recognised as either a coffee shop or a restaurant; from the time, I guessed the latter. She carried on shouting over the noise but with little success; eventually I hung up. Caleb was home without Tuesday or The Redhead and, frankly, Mary was intruding. He'd been ironing what looked like work shirts for forty minutes; the ironing board propped up in the living room to give him a good view of the television. I was part way through typing a text to tell Mary I was busy when she called again.

'Mare, I can hardly hear you,' I answered as the call connected.

'I'm outside.' She sounded unimpressed. 'Are you late, or...'

It was or. Or did you forget? Or did you lose a day? Or did you get a better offer?

'Shit, I'm so sorry–'

'Did you stand me up, is that what's happening here?'

Her tone was so hard around the edges, I felt a sudden pang

of sympathy for any man who may at one point or another have stood Mary up for dinner.

'That isn't what happened, honestly.' I was starting to throw that word around more often; usually when it wasn't in the least bit applicable. 'It was the worst day and I got home and crashed, I just completely lost track of time. Gimme ten minutes, would you?'

'Ten minutes, that's all it'll take to get ready for a date with me?'

Friend date, I thought, but the correction didn't seem likely to help. 'Dinner's on me.'

She fell silent. Mary and I had never had any huge disagreements in our friendship. But in my experience of the minor disagreements, food never made a problem worse. 'Fine, whatever, you can buy me dinner.'

'I'll be out the house in ten minutes, I promise.'

'You better be.'

'I know I'm in no position, but could you do me a favour?'

She sighed. 'You're right. But what?'

'Text me the restaurant that you're at?'

When I arrived Mary was looking around the room. She was, I guessed, playing a game of How Many Dates? but she didn't look to be enjoying it much. I pulled out the seat opposite her and for a full twenty seconds she pretended that she hadn't noticed me. Then her eyes widened and her head jerked back, feigning surprise.

'Oh, it's you.' She set her glass down. 'What a surprise, I didn't think I'd see–'

'Jesus, if I throw in dessert with dinner can you spare me?'

She softened then. 'What's going on?'

'Nothing, really.' I was already looking at the menu. Mary had been there long enough to know every item by its listed number, so I needed to make a hasty decision. 'It's just been one long day after another.'

She lowered her voice. 'Did you forget where we were meeting?'

'Yes.' I tried to laugh it off. 'Because I didn't write it down, and I'm old.'

'Only as old as me and I managed to get myself here.'

'Can I take orders now?' the waiter cut in and I could have tipped him for it.

'I'll take beer-battered cod with twice-cooked chips, and I'd like a side of onion rings, and I'd like another Sex on the Beach.' Mary stared at me the whole time she was ordering, as though underscoring how much preparation time she'd had.

'I'll have the same.'

'Two portions of onion rings?' the waiter checked, and I glanced at Mary.

'Well I'm not sharing.'

'Please, good man, two portions.' He disappeared and I wanted to collar him back just for the company – or to be a witness. 'How many apologies will this take?'

Mary rolled her eyes. 'None. But I'm worried.'

'Don't be? It's a mad time at work, really, that's all this is.'

'Are you still taking your meds?' she asked and like a knee-jerk reaction my eyes widened. 'You can't blame a girl.'

'I'm thirty minutes late for dinner and suddenly I'm crazy?'

'Ah,' she held a finger up in protest, 'I told you we don't use that word.'

I hadn't been to counselling since I'd rediscovered Fern. The conversation with Mum was the closest I'd come to openly discussing things. And I was actively avoiding conversations with Dad, so I hadn't had the chance to get his memories from it all. Fern was before Mary's time, I knew, but the thought of talking it all through caused an ache in my chest that made me realise how much I was holding in.

'You know I struggle with memory sometimes?' It was rhetorical. Mary knew because Mary had seen it. Her boyfriend in our second year of university had become abusive one night after too many drinks – 'You're a selfish bitch!' – and he bawled the house down. I bawled back, Mary said, as though he'd triggered something. They broke up shortly after – she chose me over him, naturally – but we never really talked about what happened. 'I've started to get some things back, I think.'

Mary's jaw jutted from one side to the other as though chewing over the revelation. 'Some things, meaning, memories?'

'I think so? But,' I rested my elbows on the table and leaned in, 'they're all wrong.'

'Wrong how?' She looked concerned again, and I was relieved she'd softened for this.

'I can't make sense of them, like, at all. They're in short sharp bursts and I kind of recognise things but there's a woman who I don't recognise at all, and I can't work out whether she belongs in the memories or not.' It all came out in a rush. When I looked up Mary had a raised eyebrow that made me uncomfortable. 'Don't look at me like that.'

'Who's the woman?'

I half-laughed. 'Jealous?'

Mary cracked a smile and reached out to me. There was something comforting about a hand hold; the type of contact I missed.

'It makes sense that stuff doesn't make sense, okay? These are things you misplaced years ago and, let's say, they've been in this box and now you're finally getting them out to give them a good airing. You'd expect some dust from that, right? Plus, when things have been in a box for years, they might look different when you shake 'em all out. Like, a pattern you'd forgotten about, or maybe the blue wasn't as bright as you remember it being.'

I smirked. 'We're talking about memories?'

'Yes.' She cocked the eyebrow again which at least made me smile. 'I'm just saying, don't go all *Nutty Professor* on me because you're remembering things in a different shape. Maybe they just need a good shake out, that's all.'

I squeezed her hand. 'I don't deserve you.'

'I know.'

'Sex on the Beach?' the waiter interrupted again and even he seemed more relaxed by our conciliation. I wondered whether we'd given him the air of a couple on the brink of an argument.

'Oof, please.' Mary winked at me.

I let go of her hand so she could take her drink. Her hair was wild; the flawless sort of wild that only women as loud and as beautiful as Mary can get away with. She was wearing a chiffon dress made up from a patchwork of colours: rustic orange and turquoise blue, a pink that was trying to be purple. There was a shawl thrown over the back of her chair, too; black, I thought, or at least a very dark navy blue. She sipped her drink through a straw and looked around the room, as though picking a target for us. I watched her, and I tried very hard to remember everything about the moment.

THERAPY

Claiming a mis-memory is too convenient for my liking.

I went back and forth on whether the recalls were correct or not. There had been partners of mine in the past who used 'misremembering' like a punchline to a terrible joke: forgetting a special occasion; skipping an anniversary dinner; calling me back. To rely on it for Fern felt like a weak excuse but no matter how many metronome balls I listened to, I still couldn't get further than I had the first time. So I wrapped the memories up in lined paper and carried them carefully to my counselling session, hoping that Isaac might recognise something of the mess I'd brought him. The wait to be called in was longer than I could ever remember it being – but that suddenly didn't count for much.

'He's ready for you now,' the receptionist announced, as though Isaac had called through telepathically. I scooted around her, afraid for my thoughts, and knocked on the door to Isaac's room.

'Come on in,' he shouted, somehow still using a soft voice with it. When I walked in he was sitting at his desk, surrounded by paperwork. From the stacks and slips and scribblings, I hoped it hadn't been my case he was looking through. He noted something in my expression and smiled. 'Nothing to do with you, don't worry. Shall we?' He gestured towards the comfortable chairs. There was something soothing about the space, but I still gripped my notes as though they were a licence to stay alive. 'You've brought something?'

'Notes.'

'I see.' He grabbed his pen and paper that had been waiting on the table next to him. 'Notes from the homework?'

I nodded. 'I'm a bit confused.'

'That can happen with memory recall exercises. Like we discussed.'

Had we? I narrowed my eyes, searched – somewhere. But I couldn't find the conversation he might have been referring to. 'I'm sorry, I'm sorry, I don't–'

He held a hand up to pause me. 'It's okay. It was a difficult conversation. Why don't you show me what you've brought, and we can go from there?'

I fanned the notes out, partly over my trembling knees and partly over the spare seat alongside me. Rather than hand the evidence over, I wanted to talk through it as best as I could; I knew when to censor myself while speaking. Isaac listened while I explained the patchwork – 'And then there are results, but I don't know what the results are from.' – and he made his own notes too, only pausing when I got to the best bit: 'There's a woman who I don't even recognise, but she's in every single memory. Not memory, but mis-memory. You know what I mean.' I set a hand flat on my head, as though I might be able to hold things together – or in. 'Do you know what I mean?'

He set his paper down and inched forwards in his chair. 'I think it might be helpful if we had a little talk about memories. Would that be okay?' I didn't like his tone, and I sensed the question was rhetorical. 'Some schools of thought teach us that memories are either internal or external. So, when a memory is external, we're recalling a real experience that happened to us, largely as it happened. But when a memory is internal, we're actually imagining a memory, rather than re-experiencing things how they really were. Does this sound familiar at all, or does this feel fresh?'

'Fresh.' I didn't even need to think about the answer. I could tell from the way my mind was stretching and yawning, trying to accommodate this new idea, that it wasn't knowledge I had – or at least, could remember having.

'Okay, so an external memory, let's say, could be the act of eating. But the internal memory might be the thought of eating, or an imagined version of eating. Sometimes, especially when we're using mindfulness and meditation for memory recall, either of these memory types can be stirred up.' He paused for a second as though trying to gauge my understanding, so I flashed a tight smile. 'But when these memory types happen, if one memory type closely resembles the other, so if our imagined version of eating something is really close to our actual memory of it, sometimes there might be a little bleed through between memory types.'

I tried – God how I tried – to piece everything together. But Isaac interrupted.

'You're imagining the act of eating vanilla ice cream in a restaurant, that's an internal memory. Your external memory might be the time you ate vanilla ice cream at Benedicto's. If memory one has music playing, that music might appear in memory two, even though the actual memory has no music at all.'

And then it clicked. 'So, I'm remembering the right thing, but the wrong version?'

'That would be a way of looking at it, sure.' He sat back in his seat. I wanted to ask what other fucking way someone might look at it, but I sensed my tone might ruin the moment of our breakthrough. 'We can retrieve long forgotten items by using meditation.'

'I don't remember Fern, like, at all.'

'And you've no idea who the other woman might be?'

In every memory she'd looked terribly sad; the empty kind of sadness that comes with loss or grieving. I couldn't remember that shade of love on any of the grown-ups I'd known as a teenager. 'I can't place her, and I can't think where I would have come across someone like that. Not least in a way that has anything to do with these.' I gestured at the papers.

'Consider the recalls as a framework, okay? You don't need to focus on these moments but these *types* of moments. Don't consider this exact drunken endeavour as a teenager, but think broadly and see which memory comes.'

'I thought I needed to focus on something specific?' I quoted him back from an earlier session; that much I could remember.

'You did, to find a memory. But now we have more detailed experiences to work with, and we can assume there's some significance to a drunken evening during your teens. Otherwise, why would you have blocked it out?'

Sensical it may have been, but I still couldn't find sense enough not to crumble under the weight of it all. I dug my elbows into my thighs, leaned forward and cradled my head. Isaac shifted forward, too, I heard, and his feet encroached on my view of the ground. I tried to practise breathing – deep pulls in, counting on the pushes out – because otherwise it was all going to be a conversation that we lost – again. And who's got time for that?

'Are you okay?'

'How should I know?' On my next hard exhale, I lifted myself upright and locked eyes with Isaac. 'So, my new specific is one of the experiences I've sort of remembered. But, when and if it works, I might not actually remember the same memory again, but a different stressful drunken night, or test result, or an argument with Dad? That's about it, right?'

Isaac flashed a sad smile. 'Memory recall isn't easy, I know. Did anyone say it was?'

I dropped back against my seat. 'Again, how should I know?'

He laughed. 'I promise we'll lift the veil, we just need to keep working at it for a while.'

'Which would be fine if I weren't remembering – nothing.'

'Look, I'm going to book you in for a session next week, would that be okay?'

I stared hard to try to see into him. 'Are you worried?'

'No, I'm curious. Try the memory recall again.' I knew it wasn't a question, but I nodded all the same. 'And call your doctor. I think it might be worth getting your medication increased, just slightly.' He indicated a small measurement with his finger and thumb, as though coaxing a child to eat more of their dinner; or coaxing a nutcase to swallow their pills.

'But I've felt fine,' I protested, 'with anxiety, stress, I mean. Just fine.'

He shrugged. 'Okay, but there's no harm in trying to keep it that way.'

I understood the kind reasoning. But something about an increase felt less like a 'just in case' and more like a promise that things were likely to get worse.

DOCTOR

You don't have to take every piece of advice you're given.

I called my doctors' surgery six times the day after my counselling appointment. Every time I would wait for the receptionist to answer – 'Good morning/afternoon, Brackbury's Medical Practice, how can I help you?' – before I hung up and knocked my phone into airplane mode, just in case he were to hit redial and call me back. I'd started to feel like a lovesick teenager in the throes of nervous passion, unable to get a phone call to the finish line. That first night I told myself I needed to sleep on things; in the morning I called and hung up. When I at last did manage to make conversation with the receptionist, he said, 'The doctor will have to call you back, I'm afraid, is this the best number for you?'

I eyed the clock on my living room wall. 'It is, do you have any idea when he might call?'

'The best I can do is put you down for the morning clinic. That means any time.'

'Any time this morning?'

He huffed. 'Yes.'

His tone was so curt that it crossed my mind he might know it had been me calling and hanging up on him. 'Okay, thank you for your help. Have a nice day.' I disconnected the call before he had a chance to lie to me about hoping I had a nice day too.

On the journey to work I kept my headphones in and my phone on loud. There was a staff meeting pencilled in for later in the morning, even though it wasn't the usual day for one – I checked, twice. But the rumour mill guessed that there was some big news coming our way; it seemed an obvious prediction, but I'd murmured along in all the right places during the coffee machine talk the day before. If the doctor called mid-meeting then–

The phone squealed in my ears and I answered without checking the caller.

'Hello?'

'Hey beaut, it's me.' Mary.

'Hey, is everything okay? It's early.'

'I can get up early if I want.' She sounded proud. 'I'm just checking in.'

Mary never just checked in. 'What's wrong?'

There was a long pause where I imagined her weighing up whether to be honest or whether to humour me with a grey lie. 'I'm worried about you,' she admitted. 'You really didn't seem yourself the other night.'

'I told you, I'm fine. The guy I'm seeing is frustrating the life out of me,' I said, and I really meant it, 'but I had my counselling appointment, which helped, and now I'm waiting on a callback from the doctor about tablets.' I sensed an opportunity. 'Oh shit, he's calling, Mary, I'm sorry I have to go.'

'Okay, okay, call me la–'

I reasoned that by later she'd have found something else to worry about.

~

Gladis sat at the head of the room with us crowded around like hungry schoolchildren, some on seats and others – like me – loitering at the back. She waited until there was a dead silence before she cleared her throat; she looked down at the paperwork in front of her like she'd forgotten why she'd called us here.

'I have an announcement I'd like to make which I imagine will have positive repercussions for most of the firm, which is why you've all been asked to attend. There will be some opportunities out of this that some of you might like to know about now, so you can ready yourselves.' She flashed a smug sort of smile and I wondered how much she was enjoying laying out this bait for us. It felt like the grown-up equivalent of a young adult novel; career-hungry twenty-somethings set against each other in a battle for a bigger desk. 'As of yesterday, we are representing Baker Mitchell.'

But this *was* big news. Baker Mitchell was a celebrity in commercial fiction. He wrote everything from crime to noir to romantic comedies making him an all-round threat and asset. But I didn't know what this had to do with me.

'We'll be looking to do a big social media splash to announce Mr Mitchell–'

Ah, I thought, *there I am.*

Gladis looked as though she were about to address me directly. But the thrum of my mobile vibrating in my pocket forced me to break eye contact with her. I made my apologies to everyone and no one all at once while I tried to shuffle out of the room. I could feel my cheeks redden at the disruption I'd caused.

'Hello?'

'Hi there, it's Dr Greenstone calling. Is now a good time to talk?'

It seemed a redundant question to ask after the interruption. 'Of course, absolutely, thanks for calling me.'

'No bother there. What is it I can help you with?'

I lowered my voice. 'I was hoping to discuss the possibility of upping my medication.' I stopped as though this alone were enough information for her to go on. 'Sorry, I spoke to my counsellor about it, and he recommended that I talk to you about upping my dosage for the foreseeable.'

'I see. Did he outline a reason for that?'

'I'm going through a series of memory recall exercises. I think he suspects there are some upsetting times ahead.' I tried to sound light-hearted but something about admitting it all aloud to a fresh stranger brought home the weight of it. I leaned back against the nearest wall to steady myself. 'I don't feel especially agitated at the minute.'

'Generally, though, do you feel more agitated in yourself?'

'No, I wouldn't say so.'

'Is your sleeping okay?'

I was tired most mornings, but wasn't every adult? 'Fine, as far as I'm aware.'

I could hear her thinking. 'I don't know that I'm entirely comfortable with upping your meds over the phone, it has to be said.' There were the clicks and scrolls of a mouse in the background, and I imagined her reading through my notes. 'There can be some quite serious side effects with Sertaline, you do know? Including memory problems?'

She may as well have punched me. 'I'm sorry?'

'Memory problems,' she said, slowly, as though I hadn't heard her. 'Confusion, problems thinking, even suicidal thoughts. Have you had anything like this during your time on the medication?'

'No, no, I've been fine.' But 'memory problems' rang in my head like a gong sounding. *How easy would it be*, I wondered, *to brush all of this off as a non-problem caused by meds; to pretend that none of it were abnormal at all?* 'I'm experiencing memory problems but they pre-date my time taking the medication,' I admitted. 'It's what I'm in counselling for.'

'Do you feel the counselling is working?'

'It's hard to say.' Out the corner of my eye I saw Wendy leave the meeting room. 'I think there will be some long-term benefits if I can get through these teething problems.'

More scrolls and another click. 'Are you able to get here for an appointment today?'

The temperature in my cheeks rose; I imagined two blushed spots that Wendy might claim responsibility for. 'What time today?'

'One thirty? We'll pop you before the afternoon clinic. The appointment shouldn't take long, but I do want to give you a once-over before we look at increasing your–'

'Okay,' I cut across her. Wendy was closing the distance between us. She set a hand on my shoulder and when I looked at her she mouthed, 'Everything okay?' I nodded furiously in response to her and the doctor at once. 'Absolutely,' I answered them both, 'absolutely okay, that's fine.'

'Oh-kay then.' She lingered over her syllables. 'I'll see you at lunchtime.'

'Great, thanks.' I disconnected the call and stashed my phone away in a hurry, as though hiding contraband. It might not have been my best move to act aggravated towards the woman with the magic pills, though, so I'd have to work on that during my actual appointment. 'Wendy,' I stepped away from her, 'are you okay?'

'I'm fine, are you? You left in a rush. I was worried.'

I tried to smooth out a frown. *But you don't have a right to be worried.* 'You really don't have a reason to be,' I said instead.

'Estate agents, when they call back you really have to rush and answer before it's too late.' I laughed.

'You're moving?'

'Not quite,' I said, and the lie came easily. 'I'm just hoping to look around a new flat, better views, but it's only in the building opposite to mine.'

DINNER

Some days you need to give yourself a treat just for getting to the end of it.

There hadn't been any more confrontations with Wendy – or anyone else in the office, in fact. Still, there was something inescapably long about the whole day. Mary had sucked up my lunchtime by asking whether my medication had been increased, whether I was taking the increase, whether I was free any time next week because she was seeing someone. She was relentless with her appetite – for men, life, me – and it was wearing. I'd told her I was busy – 'I'm seeing people too, you know?' – and that I'd be in touch. Between these two main female characters, the day had slipped by in dodging and question-answering; the small pockets typically reserved for me – let's say, for instance my lunch hour – had slipped by the wayside. So, on powering down the desktop and departing for the day, I took the long route home and stopped for dinner.

Clive's Bistro was downmarket in name but upmarket in appearance. The whole place was lit by unforgiving overhead bulbs that were bare in a way that would probably be described as rustic. The copper pipework and exposed brickwork only added to the feel. Although it looked like the sort of place that Mum would refer to as 'unfinished'. I got there early enough to get a table without waiting, or having booked, and I asked for a corner spot somewhere – 'Out of the way.' – where dinner with my e-reader wouldn't be disturbed.

'Of course, just this way,' said the beautiful waitress – and she was beautiful. 'Long day?' she asked, setting my menu down on a table of two.

'Aren't they all?' I half-laughed.

'Well, the days working here can feel it.' She forced a smile while I shrugged off my coat and hung it over my seat. 'Can I get you a drink, or would you like to look over the menu first?'

'Can I get a pot of Earl Grey?' I lowered my voice. 'Is that trendy enough for here?'

Her smile seemed more sincere then. 'Lemon or milk?'

'Lemon, please.'

She disappeared with a curt nod and I took a seat. The table really was cornered away, giving me a good view of most of the other tables in the room. I didn't bother with my e-reader to begin with – I only watched. When the waitress reappeared with a tray, a teapot and a warmed cup, she left without even asking about my dinner choice and I wondered how obvious I was being in my survey of the room. I picked the menu up as a courtesy then, instead looking over the top lip of it in a way that a sleuth from a black-and-white movie might have done once. It helped to imagine myself as that – someone paid to be watching. *If only*, I thought, finally lowering the menu to view.

A few minutes passed and she approached the table again, taking gentle steps as though trying not to startle me. 'Any thoughts on a dinner order? You want to get in before the rush.' She nodded behind her towards the doorway, where groups of office workers looked to be queueing for their entry.

'Do you ever have a quiet night?'

'In here, or generally?'

'Generally.' There had been some flirtation in her answer that I tried to match.

She almost giggled. 'When I'm lucky. Dinner?'

'Of course. Can I get prawn linguine?' I handed the menu back. 'A side of sourdough with butter would be great, too, please, and a Diet Coke. There's no rush with the drink, though, just whenever the food is ready.'

'Efficient.' She took the sheet. 'I like it. I'll sort out that drink when I bring your food.'

I wished I'd asked to keep the menu, feigned an interest in dessert long enough to keep my covering. Instead I pulled my e-reader out to at least create the illusion that I was busy with something. With my elbows balanced on the table, I could hold the tablet in a way that still afforded me a view of the door. So I watched as the masses poured in; a healthy mixture of couples meeting for dinner and co-workers having drinks. It was the calmest I'd felt all day and for the first time in a short while I was grateful just to have my thoughts for company. The time since Fern, since therapy, had been a struggle. While I'd tried to bring myself back to another memory recall, I knew I wasn't ready to give it the commitment it needed – and there was no point half-kicking a hornet's nest. The homework could wait another day or two, I reasoned (for the second day or two in a row).

I clicked my e-reader, ignorant to what page I was on or even whether there was a story to follow. There was a couple two tables away that I was interested in, though, because they weren't openly a couple. I mean, over the table they appeared distant and professional; yet under the table their legs were knitted together. Neither of them were wearing wedding rings, and I wondered how their not-a-real-date might unfold.

Another click and a group of women caught my eye,

huddled round a table that had been two seats short for them. 'We don't mind a bit of closeness,' one of them joked loudly with a young waiter as he brought over another seat; I could see his discomfort from a distance. When he'd gone the women occupied themselves with gossiping together and surveying the room in turns; their heads popping up like hungry meerkats whenever a new group appeared. I saw one of them nudge another and look over towards a man at the bar; maybe they were less meerkats, I thought, and something altogether more threatening.

By accident I clicked twice when my concentration slipped. I'd looked towards the door at the right moment, as though sensing the perfect newcomers. But I hadn't been expecting them at that exact time. There hadn't been anything to show when the table was booked for, or even for how many people. I'd made a lucky guess, based on recent behaviours at least, that it would only be a table for two though: '*Looking forward to a trip to @clivesbistro27 this evening for a quiet meal*'. It seemed unlikely that Caleb would be out for a quiet meal with friends, although he might have been able to convince a woman that was the case – one of his women, that is, because there could only be one that he was hoping to share a quiet night with; leaving the other home alone to read his tweet. The problem had been, during that mid-afternoon scroll through his Twitter feed, that I hadn't been able to guess at which woman it might be. It was idle curiosity – or maybe it was morbid – that had spurred me on, on the off-chance we might all be here at once. And then I saw him walk in: his tie loosened; his hair ruffled from a day of stressful dealings; and his Tuesday girl, gripped to his arm like a designer accessory – or a vice.

HOMEWORK

U nfortunately, there is a great deal of truth to: You only get out what you put in.

There was only so long I could delay a deadline, and my next appointment with Isaac was fast approaching. It gave me the excuse I needed to cancel dinner with Mum – which I hadn't been prepared for, insofar as shopping or emotions – and instead devote the evening to counselling preparation.

'Is there anything I can help with?' Mum had asked when I called.

I hesitated over the truth. 'No, Mum, I really don't think there is. But thanks.'

I went food shopping on my way home to buy the comfort I might need for when the experience was all over, though, which was the kind of self-care counselling had taught me to place value on. I had two full bags to carry back with me: one full of solace, and the other full of kale (or things that closely resembled it), because life required balance. I shouldered my way in and wasted no time in ditching the food, changing my clothes, and sitting cross-legged on the living-room floor – curtains closed to avoid all distractions. The Newton's cradle stared back at me like a worthy opponent, and I pulled the ball on the right-hand side up high and ready to drop. Before one metal curve could clang against another, though, there was a thud from somewhere behind me. I opened my eyes, to check the ball hadn't dropped without my knowing. It had been a heavy land, something muted, and I reasoned there were very few things in the place that could make such a noise.

The balls clicked together when I placed the sphere back in place. I stood up and trod out into the hallway, and the culprit was clear at first glance. There was a slim parcel sitting inside my front door and a strip of paper sticking out from the lip of my letter box: '*Rang bell, no answer*', it said, which was bollocks if ever I'd read it. I hadn't been anywhere near mindful enough to have missed a package being delivered. I collected the item and scanned the front of it for signs of a company: Global Bks Ltd looked to be the source. It was my name, and my address, of course. But I was stumped on what was inside.

From the walk between front door and kitchen I held the item loosely and tried to remember whether I'd treated myself to anything of late. The only things I was expecting had already been delivered. So, while the kettle whistled to a boil, I ripped into the cardboard outer of the packet to get to the juicy underneath. And then I stared back at the face of Fern Norton.

The book fell from my hands and landed with a heavy pound against my foot.

'Fuck it.'

Even from the kitchen floor she looked back at me. I tried to consider it a positive thing, that at least from this angle – in this image – I could remember her face. But I didn't understand the delivery still. *Looking through the ferns: The Fern Norton case* stayed stock still on the ground while I trod around it to make my tea, stepping over it dramatically as though it were ten times its actual size – which is how it felt. It wasn't until I'd made a brew – with barely any milk because I needed the hard strength of the drink – that I managed to convince myself to pick up the hardback and take it to the sofa.

The back cover described it as a close look at the outer workings of the case and the inner workings of the family. It boasted interviews with the detective team involved, outsiders from the case – whatever that meant – and one-to-one chats with close friends (although those one-to-one chats hardly suited their definitions now someone had published them in a read-all for anyone interested). But who was interested?

I edited the question: Who knew I was interested?

Mum would have forewarned me, and Wendy didn't know my home address – I hoped. It wasn't the sort of thing Isaac was likely to do; not if he valued his career, at least, which I had to assume he did. After ruling out the most likely suspects, then, there was only one terrifying option left.

I reached over to grab my laptop and hurried in my password. The desktop unfolded and I gulped two mouthfuls of tea, even though it was still too hot for comfortable drinking. It took another two mouthfuls and a brisk headshake before I could summon up the courage to open a browser, and key in the address for Global Books. I'd ordered from them before, that much I knew, and while the tab button automatically input my account details, I clutched harder at the hot mug while I waited for my screen to load. My Order History was two clicks away, and I felt my grip around the porcelain tighten while I navigated my way there.

There was only one entry displayed on the recently ordered page: *Looking through the ferns: The Fern Norton case.*

There was a loud crack, then, from strained cartilage, not the cup itself. I set the mug down, and my laptop, and rested my elbows on my knees; my head lolled towards my thighs. I practised my breathing – in for a set amount, out for a set amount – and reminded myself it was a stressful time.

'Such a stressful time.' In for four, out for five. 'Everyone forgets.' In for four, out for five. 'It doesn't mean anything is worse.' In for four, out for five. 'Only different.'

Minutes passed, taking the panic with it, but there was still something unsettled in my stomach. The tea was nearly cold now, so I decided I'd make another – and read. Caleb was due home late; he'd shared a post earlier that day to say there was a football match with the boys later that he was looking forward to. It looked as though he was sharing more of these personal details; or maybe I was seeing them more – checking more. I decided to make him my cut-off point for reading, that whenever he came home would be a perfectly good time to stop. Having replaced the cold-strong tea with a piping-hot-strong tea, I got back on the sofa.

Fern looked young in the picture, but there was something familiar about her face from the images I'd stashed away in the bottom of my wardrobe – judging that a safe distance at which to keep the scrapbook. I read the author's introduction, where he assured readers that everything was written to the best of his knowledge and investigative abilities, which seemed like an obvious promise for any true crime book to make. But I skipped the parts about how heartbreaking it had been for him to research Fern's young life. *Not heartbreaking enough not to publish a book about it*, I thought while I skimmed down the contents page to find the right spot for the opening chapter. Fifteen sheets later, I gaped down at the first family photograph – one of many to be featured – and there she was: the woman from my memories.

Or rather, Fern Norton's mother.

WEDDING

If you're suspicious about something, you're probably right.

The front doorbell woke me, which it normally wouldn't have done; partly because I'm a heavyweight sleeper, but mostly because I should have been awake hours before. My bedside clock showed a time two hours later than I needed to have been getting up for work, and I very soon imagined one co-worker after another standing outside waiting for me – an irrational thought in retrospect, but a logical one when you're fumbling one leg into your trousers while simultaneously thumbing through your wardrobe for an ironed shirt. I was barely buttoned up when I skidded along the laminate of the hallway, coming to a stop outside the spyhole. While I fumbled through the last of my buttons I looked through and, to my surprise and momentary delight, saw my dad waiting outside – not Wendy.

'What are you doing here?' I asked, with the door only just open.

'I was in the area.' He looked me up and down. 'Bad time?'

'Sort of, Dad, yeah. I'm late for work,' I started to back-step along the corridor and he followed, 'like, really late. Is everything okay?' I was already forcing things into my workbag:

an apple, that would pass as breakfast, and a bottle of water in place of my morning caffeine.

He laughed. 'No wonder you're burnt out. Who does office work on a Saturday?'

I froze in place. 'I'm sorry?'

'I said, no wonder you're burnt out. You're going to run yourself–'

'No, not that bit. The bit after that – Saturday?'

'Oh, I said who does office work on a Saturday.'

Without a word I trod out of the kitchen and into my bedroom, leaving my dad gormless as he lingered between doorways. My phone lit up when I hit the home screen and there it was, in bold letters: Saturday, with the date underneath and the time up above. But there were no missed calls from work to get back to.

'Kid, you okay over there?' Dad entered the room slowly, as though approaching a provoked animal. 'You look like you're having a moment.'

'Less of a moment.' I turned around. 'More like a whole day.'

The living room looked as though a small tornado had powered through the space. My mug was knocked over, the remnants of tea well-soaked into the carpet; the curtains were thrown open haphazardly, and the Newton's cradle upturned. The Fern Norton book I'd been reading was present and accounted for, but the dust jacket was torn in the top corner, and I hadn't taken the time to mark a page. It was the last thing I could remember: reading the book, waiting for Caleb – two nights ago.

'Come on, deal with this mess later,' Dad had said, already grabbing my elbow to steer me away from the scene. But I wondered what mess it was that I was going to have to deal with exactly. 'Put some comfy clothes on, I'm taking you out.'

In the bedroom I faced away from him while I changed. 'What are you doing here, sorry?'

'Christ, can't a father surprise his child with breakfast?' He tried to sound offended. 'Besides, I've got suit shopping to do and it would be good to have a second opinion. I don't want Carol to see the suit until the big day, you know?' He cleared his throat. 'You two had fun the other week, I hear?'

Here it is, I thought as I turned. 'We had a great time. It's nice that she felt the same. I'd really like it if we could spend more time together, as she's a second mum now and all.' I tried to make my voice sickly sweet and deliberately antagonistic; Dad twitched in a way that showed me it was working. 'And maybe she can help you out sometimes, you know, with how unwell I am and all.'

He sighed. 'I had a feeling that might come up. Look, kid, I don't–'

'Oh, wait. Before you make your excuse for that, maybe you can explain why Carol thinks you were with me the night before I saw her.' I'd done my research before throwing the claim; I knew he hadn't come over, because I could account for Caleb's whereabouts all too easily. 'Do you want to do this now or over breakfast?' I pushed by him.

'She thinks you're unwell because I value my time with you.' I didn't buy it, but I'd let it slide. He'd still have to account for the Friday night, and when I shot him an expectant glance, he realised it. 'I was with someone else the night before you saw Carol.'

'You should be fucking ashamed. Stick your breakfast.'

He followed me as I paced to the kitchen, then raised his voice to shout over the clang of cupboards. I wasn't looking for anything; apart from the opportunity to make a noise.

'You can't tell Carol about this, kid, it really isn't worth the hassle.'

I stopped then. 'Hassle for you or hassle for her?'

'For everyone. Look, people make mistakes. Adults make mistakes,' he repeated, leaning heavy on the word 'adults', as though I weren't old enough to appreciate the shitshow of adulthood yet. 'It's not a regular thing, with the other woman. She's just – she's an old flame and sometimes she and I get together and–'

I cut him off with a look. 'If this is going where I think it's going.'

'Your mother and I–'

'Dad! For fuck's sake. What is the matter with you?'

'I like women, kid. Who doesn't?' He met my eye but then waved away the question. 'Please don't tell Carol?'

'I speak to Mum all the time, and she's snide and judgemental about you, all the time.'

He laughed. 'She's like that with me for what it's worth.' I raised an eyebrow. 'Okay, maybe it's not worth all that much.'

'Well, at least she's consistent. Which is more than I can say for you.'

'Christ, you get your high-and-mighty mouth from your mother at least.' He raised his voice and my stomach turned. 'All I need to know is whether you're going to tell Carol about this. So, are you?' He waited a beat and then asked again, louder. 'Are you going to tell her?'

It rushed in like a wave, and its crash was just as loud: Dad shouting, asking whether I'd told her. I landed heavy against the kitchen side and gripped onto the worktop. Breaths were coming hard and fast but they didn't seem to let any air in. But I couldn't remember what he didn't want me to tell her. It occurred to me I was panting, and Dad was shouting more but I didn't know whether it was then or before. So I was shouting back and asking, begging–

'Breathe with me, kid, okay.' He had the same panic in his

voice, and I could see him with watercolour edges crouched in front of me. Dad was shouting, asking whether I'd told her, whether I could breathe for him. 'Are you going to tell her?' One question overlaid another making a medley of then and – Dad was shouting. 'People won't see it for what it was.' I was shouting back and asking, begging – 'In through your nose and out through your mouth, kid, you remember this.' I couldn't remember what he didn't want me to tell – 'Jesus, can you just help me? You're a part of this now.' I was shouting back and begging, but–

I didn't know what was then and what was before.

HIM

Sometimes a change isn't as good as a rest; sometimes, rest is the thing.

Dad left me on the sofa swathed in blankets. My panic attack – the first he'd seen me have since I was a child – had ended with me pooled on the kitchen floor, my legs suddenly liquid. He'd manhandled me from one room to another once my breathing had regulated, though, and found all the soft things he could to gather around me. He brought hot tea and placed the television controls within reaching distance, then he crouched down on his knees, so we were level.

'What happened back there?' He used his softest voice. I recognised it from bedtime stories and coaxed confessions, from when I'd taken more than my share of biscuits or confectionary from the kitchen. He always had a way of getting me to talk. 'I know I raised my voice, but – I'm sorry,' he said, as though deciding an apology might be easier than an excuse, just this once. 'Did I do something?'

I shook my head. 'I misremembered something, I think. I've been doing memory recall as part of counselling and it's brought

– well, I don't know what it's brought up. I haven't worked it out yet.'

'What are you trying to remember?' he asked, his brow furrowed.

I laughed. 'Everything I've managed to forget.'

He stood from his crouch, then, but in doing so knocked his foot against something that caused a soft clunk. Dad reached down to the offending article and pulled back up the book I'd been reading; the one about her. He looked the cover over and took a quick glance at the snippet endorsements written on the back; he looked confused.

'What are you reading this nonsense for?' He set it down out of reach. 'Is that what you're trying to remember?' Dad's voice was worried at the edges and I swallowed the small swell of panic it had caused in my belly. 'It was a terrible time; you don't want to remember it.'

'Memory recall doesn't work that way, Dad. You can't pick and choose.'

'Then maybe you shouldn't be doing it at all.' He rubbed his palm into the crown of my head. 'Is there anything else you need?'

'I just need a rest. Really, I'll be fine.'

'Shall I get your phone? You can call me if you need me?'

We both knew that wasn't true. 'My legs are fine, my arms are fine.' I waved my hands about as though in evidence. 'I can get stuff, really. I just need to sit on my arse for the day.'

'Which is what Saturdays are for.'

Once he felt like he'd fulfilled his fatherly duties he excused himself and told me to make sure I got the rest I needed. When I heard the latch of the front door click behind him, I let out a heavy sigh that I hadn't realised I was holding in. Something in his tone, in his worry, had made my stomach into a washing machine and the cycle was ongoing. I dropped my head back against the sofa, shut my eyes and counted; in for four and out for five. But I couldn't unhear the argument – worse still, I couldn't work out which argument it was.

The morning had slipped away which meant I'd missed any early glimpse at Caleb. I hadn't checked his feeds since – *when did I last check his feeds*? But he usually went out on Saturdays. It would be hours until he came home; most likely drunk, or at the very least, ready to go out and get drunk. It was a terrible habit he had, drinking so much every weekend, but he worked hard all week and it seemed unfair to criticise his one vice. Or rather, his one vice apart from juggling women – which was also a problem, admittedly.

I crept out from beneath my blanket to grab the Fern Norton biography that Dad had set out of reach, and brought it back with me to the den of the sofa. Between reading and rest, I decided, I could wait out Caleb coming home. But somewhere between chapters four and five I fell asleep, my head at a crooked angle against the arm of the sofa. When I woke up, clutching the book like a security blanket to my chest, daytime had peeled away into darkness. I couldn't guess at the time, so I stumbled out from my nest and trod to my bedroom to get my phone. There were still no missed calls; nothing from a concerned Dad, for instance, to check on my well-being.

'Worried my arse,' I said, thumbing through my social media apps to find Caleb's many feeds. I alternated glancing through his Twitter page and glancing through the shelves of my fridge, before eventually deciding there was nothing to see in either. Instead I went to the menu drawer in my kitchen and flicked through logos until I arrived at Chinese. There was nothing on his Facebook feed, apart from a message someone had left on his wall. Howie Deaver had written, '*Yo. Is your phone broken or are you ghosting us?*' and there were four likes on the note already. I didn't recognise Howie from his profile picture.

Opting against human contact, I used the FeedMe app to order my dinner for the night. When I was back on the sofa – light on and book ready – I checked Caleb's Instagram. There were no new pictures and nothing spinning in his stories section. From the viewpoint of my sofa I could see straight ahead into his living room, where there were no lights and no shuffling shadows. It crossed my mind that Caleb was doing the same as me; staring out into the city, trying out an evening of rest – although it seemed unlikely. I dropped my phone in the folds of soft fleecing and tried to retrace my steps through the book, settling on a paragraph I vaguely recognised. There was nothing else I could do, I decided, only wait – and watch.

PART IV

ME

I'm an honest person at heart. But there are dishonest things I've misplaced.

There were times when my lapses were so convenient that even I wondered whether I'd fabricated the problem. I could see why friends, family, teachers – and eventually lecturers, employers, colleagues – would think that simply forgetting an argument worked in my favour; ergo, why wouldn't I play the card at every chance? But playing a card one too many times is an obvious mistake, and I told Mum as much when she sat me down for a parental discussion one Saturday afternoon.

'Why would I keep doing it, to fake it, to make people not believe me?'

Mum narrowed her eyes. 'Why wouldn't you?'

'If you keep doing the same magic trick, sooner or later someone is either going to guess what you're doing or get bored of seeing you do it.'

'You think your memory is a magic trick?'

'No, Mum, so I wouldn't treat it like one. I don't want people to get bored of me.'

She reached and squeezed my hand. 'Honey, we're just trying to work out what happened.'

What happened? Lucas O'Reilly from two houses down was telling the girls that he'd love them forever if they'd let him see their underwear. He'd nudged me and asked me to agree, as though my encouragement would make it a done deal – but I couldn't. We were too young to be flashing our knickers and I thought Lucas knew as much. Plus, Lucas wasn't the kind of kid to keep a secret. If any of the three girls in front of us had even so much as lifted a hem it would have been around school quicker than any of us could say, 'Collective detention.' We were thirteen at the time and I tried to tell him he'd got the rest of his life to ask girls to show him their underwear, but that argument didn't fly. He pushed me and I stumbled into one of the girls, who then fell over and started crying. I remember the turn in my stomach. Lucas called me a bully; asked why I wanted to go around ruining fun and picking on people smaller than me; asked why I didn't take a hint and leave him alone.

So, I hit Lucas with the first thing that came to hand: half a house brick.

'Didn't the girls tell you what had happened?' I asked.

The girls thought I was a hero. The one I'd bumped into stopped crying and instead burst out in laughter. The hit hadn't been hard; it was enough to break the skin on his cheek and leave a little blood there afterwards, but I hadn't been stupid enough for anything more than that. Still, the three appreciated having someone stand up for them; they recognised that need for protection and solidarity early on, like I did.

'They said Lucas was pushing you and them around.'

'Right?'

'Is that how you remember it?'

I sighed. 'Mum, I just don't remember. I'm really sorry.'

'It's okay, honey.' She pulled me into a tight hug and kissed the top of my head. 'If you can't remember then you can't remember. The girls are on your side so I'm sure nothing will come of it.' She kissed the top of my head again, with more force the second time. 'I always thought that kid had a punch coming one day anyway.'

TUESDAY

Social media makes everyone that little bit more glamorous.

Tuesday's real name, Louise Sou Thackerey, was easy to track. The spelling of her middle name seemed like a conventional Sue but the consistency across all her social media – websites included – made it difficult to dispute. I had to settle for taking a personal grudge against it instead – which was easy, considering her relationship with Caleb. I'd already seen from her Twitter bio that she was a freelance media consultant, which seemed to translate to her working on lots of high-end magazines and the occasional short film. Louise was the perfect combination of intimidating – due to her job listing – but suspiciously nice – as I saw from her tweets. She looked to be a big advocate of independent artistry, having shared promotional bits and pieces for umpteen Etsy-style accounts. There was an irony, I thought, to someone in the high-flying end of the media world promoting the importance of buying from their local anything-makers. But everyone looked to lap it up because Louise's 32,076 followers were often liking, retweeting, and commenting on the things she shared. I couldn't decide whether it was her work that had got her such a high follower account, or her pretty face.

She occasionally shared pictures of her and her friends looking beautiful somewhere. The friends were always tagged, their handles listed across the bottom of the image, but their location was mentioned too. Louise, like Caleb, had a face that would lend itself well to a promotional campaign, and I wondered whether she dined out, worked out, and coffee-ed out for enjoyment or whether it was part of her monthly income. There was no telling.

The bulk of her pictures were reserved for Instagram. She had a wide-open account but also mentioned her official business account in her personal bio: *'For business enquiries you can sample my work at @lousoumedia'*. The whole account was a mess of photography shoots, online editing, and Louise looking great in a power suit. She was just the right kind of feminine for a two-piece pressed suit to look right on her and, far from butch, the whole thing made her womanliness pop. The trousers were well-tailored to show the curve of her thighs and into her hips; she always had one hand tucked into her front pocket, to strategically flash a small waistline and white T-shirt. Oh, Louise knew what she was doing.

Over on @lousoulifestyle there were just as many pictures of her looking glorious, glamorous – much more put-together than she appeared after rolling around Caleb's couch for two hours, but there was no photographic evidence of that. There were more pictures of her out with friends, either at the beach or a restaurant or at – somewhere! She led an active social lifestyle, that much was apparent from the early images. Further down, though, beyond the squares of social status, there was Louise's family. A woman who I assumed was her mother – *'Where do these good looks come from you ask?'* was the caption – who stood as tall and toned as her daughter and, yes, it was easy to see where Louise had inherited those genes from. Her mother looked as though she'd walked out of a magazine shoot and I wondered whether they'd both made a special effort for the picture, or whether that really was the normal for some people. Louise's dad – who I found seven pictures later – looked much more approachable with the waistline of a man who'd lived his life well. It was a Father's Day shot of them both – '*To the best and only man in my life!*' she'd captioned it – and I saw that it was from earlier in the year. I wondered what Caleb had made of that.

It was easy to find Louise on other social media platforms. Her Facebook profile had boasted more of the same things as her other accounts. Again, it was open to anyone. I couldn't decide whether this was irresponsible or clever. Admittedly, there were things in my life I wouldn't exactly want to tweet about, but sharing everything seemed a drastic extreme. It must have been strategic, I decided, by the time I was halfway through her yearly posts on this platform. There was nothing incriminating, embarrassing or dramatic – and a woman with Louise's beauty and status must have had some of each to share. I wondered whether there was another account locked away, detailing the sexual antics of her and Caleb, and the shortfalls of her romantic endeavours before him.

She'd been a freelance media consultant since leaving her job at Parker NewMan Imaging, which was a behind-the-scenes company dedicated to photoshopping men and their behaviours – at least, that's how their online presence made it sound. It wasn't a surprise that Louise had left an environment like that; more surprising, in fact, that she'd worked there at all. But her LinkedIn profile showed glowing recommendations, with her former colleagues endorsing her individual skills and leaving complimentary comments alongside their ratings for her. '*Watching television while having sex*' wasn't listed but I would have given her a five-star rating for it; Caleb might not have noticed, but I had.

Louise Sou Thackerey had a perfect online presence in every corner and crevice I looked in. The only mentions I could find of Caleb were friendly ones – catching up for a drink or going out for dinner. It looked as though neither of them had made themselves publicly accountable for their relationship, which I took a great deal of comfort in – it spoke volumes on their thoughts of the set-up, I thought. But no matter how hard I looked or what stone I peered under, there were certain things I couldn't find. Louise's age, for example, or any details of the last time she was in a relationship; she'd blanked the question entirely on Facebook leaving a 'No relationship information' box to take care of curious lookers.

But the thing that really stumped me, was why she'd let herself into Caleb's apartment at around lunchtime one Sunday – when he hadn't been home at all the night before.

WORK

Apologise to the beast before it asks for an apology.

I hadn't heard from anyone at work about my Friday absence, which made me feel even more guilty for it. There hadn't been a time before where I simply hadn't turned up to something – at least, not a time I could remember, which I appreciate may not count for much. But having gone a whole weekend without so much as an email – I'd given in and checked my work account in the early hours of Sunday morning – made me suspicious of colleagues, as well as myself. It occurred to me that perhaps they'd written me off entirely, that my desk might be packed away into neat little boxes when I stepped in through the office doors. But no, everything was there, including a Post-it note in Fred's handwriting: *'Emailed over Keogh, Hanson and Mullen publication timelines'*. He was the curtest of the literary agents so there weren't even any clues to be found in his address.

Over the course of the morning a number of colleagues went by, including Beverley, who even went as far as asking how my weekend had been. I tried to find something snide or suggestive in her tone, but I couldn't, no matter how hard I looked.

'It was fine, thank you,' I answered, 'although I spent most of it on the sofa.' *Post-panic attack*, I thought but didn't say because I knew this was a common courtesy conversation rather than a sincere one. 'How about yours?'

'Ah, you know.' She shrugged. *Well, I don't, which is why I asked.* 'Sometimes it's just nice not to be working, isn't it?'

'I suppose so.'

She shrugged again, signalling the end of the exchange, and then disappeared.

I couldn't wait any longer for a confrontation to arrive either on my desk or in my inbox, though, and when the office quietened for lunch I vowed to stick my head into the lioness' mouth – lest she snap while I wasn't looking. Ordinarily I wouldn't dream of approaching Gladis' office door without an appointment. But her gatekeeper – the secretary to rule all secretaries – was on her own lunch break, leaving the door unguarded. I'd knock quietly, I decided, and if she answered then – well, I'd deal with that situation when it arrived. I tapped my knuckles against the door twice and counted the seconds.

'Come in then,' she shouted.

Gladis' office was a glorious display of accomplishments, where the walls were adorned with collages of bestsellers that she'd represented throughout her years in publishing. Rumour had it there were more stashed in storage and I could believe it; in the time she'd been heading up the company, she'd already proven herself to be a machine.

'M, what can I do for you?'

I hovered by the door as though keeping a safe distance. 'I wanted to talk about Friday.'

'Come, sit,' she pointed to the seat opposite her, 'do you need the time off?'

'No, sorry, not this Friday, last Friday.' I followed her instruction to sit. There was a slim strand of fear coursing through me; the kind that forces you to comply, where neither fight nor flight seem optionable. I didn't understand what was troubling me so much; it was a simple apology, and one that was owed. 'I really wanted to apologise, if I'm honest.'

She laughed. 'For last Friday?'

'For my absence, I mean.'

'M, goodness. You had a sick day, it happens. Are you feeling better?'

I flashed back to the panic of Saturday; I'd pulled muscles in my stomach from tensing. 'I'm fine, thank you, but I realise that I–'

'You look absolutely petrified,' she stopped me, and she sounded sincerely concerned. 'Despite reputation, I'm not a dragon lady. You were sick, for goodness' sake. You called in to let the team know, and that's that.'

'I did?' She cocked an eyebrow at my question. 'I did.'

'You're sure you're well enough to be in?' She lowered her glasses. 'You look a little...' I wondered how the sentence might have ended had she continued, but I didn't give her the chance to pick up the thread.

'Really, I'm fine. Guilty conscience for letting people down, that's all.' I was up and out of the seat, back-stepping to the door as though scared to turn around on her. 'I have plenty of sick days remaining so, I know it's not really a problem. I just wanted to make my apology in person, so you knew, you know, that I felt bad.'

'Gosh,' she put her glasses back in position and glanced back at her computer, 'if only the rest of them were as concerned as you are. Speaking of which, Eleanor wants a word.'

'Right,' I opened the door, 'I'll drop her an email. Thanks again, Gladis.'

'Quite welcome.' She sounded as though I'd lost her interest already.

On Friday I checked my phone for calls from work; it had never occurred to me to check outgoing calls as well. The office was quiet enough still for my panic to bubble undisturbed, while I hurried back to my desk and searched through my bag for my mobile. Both of my parents had been calling me alternately since Dad's revelation at the weekend; my missed calls list was crammed with their numbers, and I wondered whether they'd drawn up a rota for trying to get in touch with me. Mum had left another voicemail, but I sidestepped it for the sake of getting to my outgoing calls. Under the small phone icon with an arrow pointing outward I scrolled back to Friday morning; I didn't exactly have far to go. And then I saw it – one quick phone call at the crack of opening hours, lasting one minute and thirty-seven seconds.

THERAPY

Defending your behaviour from the start is a good plan of attack.

Isaac sat opposite me with a pen and paper in hand. This was my emergency appointment – we weren't calling it that, but that's what it was. He'd come out into the reception space to meet me personally, something he'd never done before, and guided me into his room with a sympathetic frown and a head tilt – as though he were on the cusp of asking how I was, but feared others might hear the answer. Before he had the opportunity to launch into whatever he'd noted down on his pad already, I initiated a talk.

'I haven't done another memory exercise.'

He sighed, gently, but I noticed. 'Okay,' he sat the pen and paper down, 'why's that?'

'They're quite difficult, you know?' I sounded petulant even to myself and from Isaac's expression it was clear he'd noted the tone. 'I'm sorry, it's just – well, they're really difficult.'

'More or less difficult than walking around without memories forever?'

I laughed. 'How can I even answer that question?'

'Only one way to find out,' he replied, with the smugness of a parent. I tipped my head back and stared at the ceiling, as though another client-patient might have scribbled an escape route there. 'Why don't we start by talking about the last week generally? Ease in.'

When I looked back at him, everything poured forth. I gushed about my parents and the irresponsibility of their behaviour; my frustration, more than anything, at being centred in their behaviour. Mum had left sixteen voicemails in the space of two days while Dad had left only one – 'Your mother is worried. Call her.' – which seemed to sum up our entire family dynamic in one clean incident. I'd typed texts to them both that I hadn't urged myself into sending, but I hadn't arrived at a point of returning their calls.

'Is the problem that they're sleeping together, or that they're lying about it?'

I thought hard and then said, 'Yes.'

'You want them to be open about their behaviours?'

'Accountable.' I spat the word out without thinking too much about it, but it seemed an odd choice. 'I don't know what I mean by that.'

'You think they should have to answer to their behaviours.' Isaac raised an eyebrow and smiled. 'Don't we all have to answer to our behaviours at some point? If we've done something, if we remember doing something that we perhaps shouldn't have done.' He leaned hard on the word 'remember'; there was nothing subtle in his meaning.

'It's different doing something wrong and knowing it's wrong.'

'I'm not saying you've done anything wrong. I'm suggesting that, maybe, we don't always want to face up to things that have happened, and denial is a way of managing that.'

'You think I'm in denial?'

'Do you?'

I hated when he did that although I knew it was what I was paying him for. 'Yes.' We were both quiet for a beat. 'Yes, I'm in denial about things that happened, and not remembering them makes it easier for that denial. But Christ, doesn't everyone deny things?' I snapped.

'Yes, they do.'

He waited for the penny to drop. 'It still doesn't excuse their behaviour.'

Isaac reached over and wrote something down. 'How's the medication change?'

It had only been a few days and already I was feeling the effects of changing my tablets, or rather, increasing them. They weren't making me less anxious so much as they were making me feel nauseous and bloated and like I might need a bathroom at any minute of the day. Taking them first thing in the morning had always been helpful for sleep disturbances; but now I found myself pacing the floors at all hours, staring out to watch the city. There were the headaches, too, that no amount of ibuprofen would kick.

'You seem agitated,' he added when I didn't answer. 'Increases can do that sometimes.'

'I don't know that it's the medication,' I admitted. What I meant was that I absolutely knew it wasn't the medication. The thing that had set me on edge was missing time, which I still hadn't been able to place. Plus, Caleb must have been on a new work-social schedule because seeing him was an impossibility too. I didn't know which thing grieved me worse.

'Has something happened?'

I opened my mouth to answer but it felt a terrible thing to admit aloud.

Isaac flashed a sad smile and continued, 'What is it you want to be getting out of these sessions going forwards?' He held a palm up to stop me from answering. 'Maybe that's something you can think about between now and our next talk. These sessions are meant to be helping you with your difficulties in remembering things. Talking about the day-to-day incidents are fine, of course. But they're not really why you're here.'

This was the you're-not-letting-me-down talk that parents and teachers usually reserved for their worst students. But never in my life had I been a bad student so, fuelled by spite, I think, I said, 'I lost a chuck of time at the end of last week. Friday. August 7th.' I'd starred the date in my diary.

'Lost, in terms of your memory?'

'Yes.' I shifted uncomfortably. 'I was reading a book about the girl, the one who was murdered when I was a teenager. The last thing I remember is reading that book on the sofa; there was tea,' I added, as though this were an important detail. 'The next thing I can remember is Dad hammering on my door on Saturday morning, while I'm rushing around to get ready for work, because I was under the impression it was Friday. I thought I'd overslept, I suppose, from Thursday night.'

He noted down an awful lot from the confession then asked, 'What happened with work? No one called you in your absence?'

'Whatever I was doing I was functional because I called them.'

'To forewarn them of your absence?'

'I called to tell them I was sick, and I needed the day off.'

He narrowed his eyes. 'But you don't believe that to be true?'

Like seeing an old photograph, my head flickered back to an image of the dishevelled living room, the spilt tea and the torn corner of the book. 'No,' I admitted, defeated. 'No I don't believe that to be true. I think something happened.'

'Something – like what?'

Something bad, I didn't reply. But somehow, I just knew.

DINNER

Taking annual leave is sometimes the last thing your brain needs.

Two days after counselling I decided I wanted to stay in bed all day. I knew it was a bad sign. But the day before, when I'd been in work, I'd blocked out my calendar and booked a day's holiday. I reasoned it wasn't quite as bad to spend a day in bed if I'd planned ahead for it; it's not like I just gave up one morning – although I wasn't ruling it out. Since seeing Isaac – since admitting things aloud – there had been a pile-up of worries that concertinaed into each other, making it difficult to know where to start. We'd decided that what I wanted from the sessions was to retrace my memories, though, so at least we'd made progress in terms of why I was still paying him an inordinate amount to spend time with me. To spend so much money and not even get sexual gratification at the end of it though; it was something worth thinking about (it was a half-joke but there was definitely something serious in the thought). He'd asked me to try memory recall on my own before the next appointment, and we'd arrange for a follow-up in a week's time.

'We aren't dropping back to every two weeks?' I said as he filled in his diary space.

'Do you think we should?'

I let him have that one and agreed to an appointment.

My annual leave was spent drifting in and out of a restless sleep for most of the morning. It felt as though my thoughts sat somewhere between dreams and memories, and I couldn't tell whether Dad was shouting at me or whether I'd turned up for work naked again. After three hours of it, I decided it might be worth getting out of bed after all. I looked across Caleb's living room and there she was – Tuesday, even though it wasn't her day. She was scouting around the room for something, opening drawers and slamming them closed again. For the last couple of days she'd done this; appeared now and then for a look around. It was always while Caleb was out, and I began to wonder whether she'd heard about The Redhead – or at least had her suspicions. Whatever the reason, it felt like an invasion of privacy on her part. I'd thought better.

I hadn't made an effort to catch Caleb since my appointment with Isaac; I'd thrown the occasional glance across, sometimes to see Tuesday and sometimes to see nothing at all. But as part of my day off I at least wanted us to have dinner. While Tuesday snooped, I started to run a bath, determined that a long soak would be a better use of a day away from the office, while giving me time to consider menu options.

The water steamed and my skin flushed red as I lowered myself in to soak. There was chicken in the fridge; peppers that probably needed to be used; I had enough ingredients to make couscous. Our playlist hummed in the background but midway through our Smashing Pumpkins classic the sound cut out, replaced by the buzz of an incoming call. I peered over the edge of the bath and saw it was Mum. Isaac had urged me to talk to at least one of my parents in the week between appointments, too, and this was at least easier than the memory recall. I leaned over to swipe an answer and clicked my phone on loud.

'Finally,' Mum burst through the speaker, 'haven't you been getting my messages?'

'Yeah, Mum, I've just been ignoring them.'

'Now, come on. This isn't like you, you always talk to me.'

'This isn't like you,' I answered back, accompanied with a splash as I pulled water over my face. 'What are you doing messing around with him?'

'That's all it is, honey, we're just messing around.'

'But Carol–'

'I know, I know,' she interrupted me. 'Look...'

I didn't look; I didn't listen. I placed a palm flat on my stomach where I imagined I could feel a ball of stress forming, a physical shift. Would I even remember this?

'Mum, stop whatever you're trying to say.' I used a curt voice as though interrupting her, but I wasn't sure she'd even been talking still. 'What you and Dad do is your business. I think it's a shitty thing to do, but it's my business to think that. Why don't we leave it there?'

She sounded flummoxed in her agreement. 'Of course. If that's what you want.'

We left the call on good terms. But she ruined my bath.

From process of elimination just by sell-by date, I decided that dinner would be garlic chicken with steamed vegetables. It wouldn't be the most filling, but there was a tub of white chocolate ice cream in the freezer that I'd been shamelessly flirting with for some days, and that would make a good dessert. While the chicken boiled and burst and bubbled, the garlic sauce rising around it, I set about rearranging the living room. I slotted the dining table beneath the window ledge and laid it out for one, looking out over the city – not that the city mattered.

There was still a good half an hour before Caleb would

arrive home – although he hadn't exactly been keeping to times, still I resolved to take my chances. It left me with enough time to try on seven different outfits – everything from plain T-shirts to fitted, button-up shirts to an overpriced designer one that I couldn't even remember buying. On any given evening I might have decided on comfort, on a day off too. But after not seeing him for days it felt like I should make the effort, so I slipped on the overpriced shirt and admired myself in the mirror. It was the wrong fit, though, and the wrong colour and – wrong! The timer clicked over in the kitchen leaving me no time to change back into outfit number two which, as anyone can attest to, is usually the best of the bunch.

The kitchen stank of garlic and I was grateful for the distance from my living room to Caleb's – just this once. I plated everything up and set the leftovers aside to cool; before the evening was out I'd snack on whatever vegetables were left – at least the shirt left size for that.

In the living room I set the plate down and caught sight of myself in the mirror. *Why do I have so many mirrors around?* I had to fight back on the urge to change. Dinner would go cold, I reasoned, and Caleb could be home any minute.

From my peripheral vision I saw a light snap on in his living room. The shirt would have to do, I decided, as I pulled out my chair and took a seat at the makeshift mealtime. I cut into the chicken absent-mindedly, with my attention fixed on the window opposite; my heart rate increased to the point that I could feel a dull thump. Sampling a mouthful, I threw the meat around like a teenager eating popcorn, but my second cut into it was disturbed. With knife and fork poised either side of the breast, I watched as Tuesday walked into Caleb's living room again – only this time she wasn't alone.

This time there was a man behind her. The new man's shirt fit just right; a crisp white that stood out around the deep black body armour. The man looked around the room as he walked. Soon there was another person, though, a woman who came to stand behind the man; she said something to him as she came in. The woman wore a clean white shirt too. And they both wore bright silver badges.

HIM

The media outlets will drive you mad if you let them.

It was two days before anything was considered newsworthy. In that time there were people traipsing in and out of Caleb's apartment with worrying regularity; they gave me so much to watch but left nothing to see. The officers took away all manner of personal effects as though they were part of an extreme decorating crew. The majority of them wore uniforms that I recognised from living in a busy city; I wasn't a stranger to the police force, although I'd always been on the right side of it. There was a woman, though, who didn't wear uniform. Whenever she entered the room there was a shift in everyone around her, and she seemed to enter the room a lot.

In this time I convinced myself that Caleb had done something wrong – that the police were in fact looking for evidence of ill-gotten gains that they could use against him in a court of law. But when the news did arrive, that wasn't quite the case.

'They're saying he's a missing person now, aren't they?' Jonathan said to the huddle of women around him one morning at work. 'That's what I heard, anyway, on the news.'

My stomach turned. I'd been checking news reports avidly. I couldn't decide whether I was frustrated at having missed something or just that Jonathan had got to Caleb first. While my coffee leaked out of the machine, I tried to convince myself they could have been talking about anyone. It didn't have to be something to do with me and Caleb, it didn't have to–

'M, isn't that the building you were viewing an apartment in?'

Wendy's voice cut through me like a shard. 'I don't know,' I lied as I turned to face them all. 'What is it that's happened?'

'Oh, some poor sod has lost her boyfriend.'

'Jonathan!' Beverley slapped his arm playfully. 'There's a young man that's gone missing in the city, M, that's all.'

Her 'that's all' was the second shard to cut into my belly. 'Missing?'

'They've combed his apartment but can't find anything to explain where he might be.' Wendy shrugged. 'Maybe he just needed a break.'

'Without taking credit cards with him?' Jonathan goaded her.

'You don't know that, Jonathan. They literally haven't said a word on it.'

He half-laughed. 'I'm just saying, when men disappear in cities like this one, and it's their girlfriends who can't find them, he's usually a jumper or a dumper.'

The women fell about themselves in mock outrage and I backed away.

'Is everything okay?' Wendy asked, somehow next to me already. 'You look...'

I smiled. 'I'm getting that a lot lately. I'm just a little under the weather, really.'

'You're sure? Do you need a walk back to your desk?'

My desk was two corridors away, but she'd managed to make

it sound like an Olympic sprint. 'I'll be fine, really.' I lifted my cup. 'This will set me straight.'

She didn't protest further, so I slipped away unharried and, back at my desk, I loaded every news outlet that came to mind. Caleb wasn't even mentioned in the majority of them and I tried to find a balance between being outraged and relieved. The first extensive coverage – if a 500-word article counts as extensive, that is – was in the *Birmingham Gossip*, of all places. They talked about high-flying businessman Caleb Neale having gone missing, how his 'friend and companion' had reported him gone. I skim-read, trying to absorb as much as I could in one go, but for a short article there was a lot to take in.

Ms Louise Thackerey (no middle name, I noted, and I wondered whether it had irked her) had reported Caleb Neale missing after two days, when she couldn't reach him at home (*nor could she find him at home*, I thought, because I knew for a fact she'd looked). Police had entered the home with Ms Thackerey – who had a key for security reasons (not just so she could beat Caleb home and be waiting naked now and then) – and found there was no suspicious evidence relating to Mr Neale, other than his prolonged absence. Police have since launched more extensive investigations (that looked a lot like turning Caleb's apartment upside down in case he was hiding under the furniture) to try to locate Mr Neale, and they're asking for anyone who might know of his whereabouts to come forward and contribute to the investigation. Due to the time passed since Mr Neale was last heard from, police are treating this as the beginnings of a missing persons case. The timeline suggests that Mr Neale hasn't been seen or heard from since his final contact with Ms Thackerey last week, on Thursday – August 6.

HOMEWORK

We forget things for a reason.

The longer I went without seeing Caleb, or hearing news of him, the greater my desperation was to claw at memories. I tried every morning and every evening, in a hurried and frantic way, to trick myself into remembering – as though if I could catch the memory by surprise it might come flooding back. But nothing did. I tried to sneak up on the memory slowly instead, then, setting the tone with a quiet flat and the godforsaken balls that would bring about a meditative state. The clang of metal on metal set a rhythm for my breathing; in – through the belly up through the lungs and back again – out – knock. It was the steadiest I'd been for days, so I took another pull of air and imagined the taste of cider and poor judgement.

I was holding a sheet of paper and I was crying but they were happy tears rather than sad – in through the belly – and Mum was there – 'We're so proud of you, love.' – and then Dad – up through the lungs – 'Honestly, kid, you've done great here.' – and the writing is blurred but the letters are big and bold – and back again out – 'These results, God, they're so good. We must celebrate, we must,' Mum said. 'Did you cheat?' someone asked – in through the belly – but I didn't recognise their voice–

Up through the lungs – and I could smell cigarette smoke but none of us were old enough – and back again out – so I don't know where it was from. But there was the campfire – in through the belly and up – and I wondered whether the smoke was coming from that – through the lungs and back – but I waved smoke away and realised someone was blowing smoke on me, into my face, as though trying – in through the belly – to block my vision and– 'Some of us tried really fucking hard, do you know that?' – up through the lungs – and it's the same voice but I don't know it – 'Fern, get out of it. You'll make up for it at A Levels.'

And back again out – 'Get down here! Get down here now, I want to bloody talk with you!' – in through the belly – and I rushed down the stairs in the family home, pounding down them with speed and I was worried that I'd wake Dad – up through the lungs and back – but she was being so loud – 'How did you do it, eh? How did you of all people manage it?' – again out and in through the belly – 'You're going to wake my dad. Just go back to your party.'

'What's happening?' Dad asked but he sounded like – sounds like someone else.

Up through the lungs – but my lungs were tight so I tried a second attempt and realised I was crying – in the memory. In through the belly – 'Kid, you need to stop crying and help me.' – up through the lungs and back. 'I bet you cheated.'

I remember all the voices at once like a montage of anger and accusation. I realised that Fern's mother wasn't there anymore, then, and I wondered how she'd been replaced. In through the belly – 'Did you cheat? Just tell me, would you?' someone asked and they got angry when I wouldn't answer – up through the lungs – I was worried about them waking someone but they weren't worried at all – and there was a shuffle, scuffle then–

'Do I know you?'

The question rang out and my chest flooded with panic and pain. My eyes snapped open and I tumbled forward, in the right time frame. I set a hand on the Newton's cradle to stop the balls from clanging although I knew that couldn't be the end of it. There were new memories and I didn't want to let them go. I'd left a notebook to hand, ready for when the panic stirred, so I reached out and wrote down as much as I could remember, writing the question in block capitals – DO I KNOW YOU – with rings wrapped around it to remind me of its importance, for when I forgot again.

When the balls clapped together – in through the belly – it didn't take long to find the thread I'd let go of. To start with it was a mess of campfires, sheets of papers, pats on the back. But I could see Fern. She was sitting opposite me with a boy wrapped around her waist and she was drunk – up through the lungs – because her eyes had that blankness that comes with booze – and back again out. As though filtered in through a faulty connection, though, the memory started to flicker. I could remember being in the back garden – in through the belly – but it was late, and freezing, and I wasn't wearing any shoes – up through the lungs – and I was scared of waking someone up but Fern didn't mind – and back again out – 'Do I know you?' In through the belly – 'They all think I've gone home,' she said but she said it with more spite than it deserved and I couldn't remember what I said to deserve it – up through the lungs. 'Can we do this another time, please?' I asked and I turned and she laughed at me – in through the belly – 'We're going to wake my dad.' She couldn't even focus on me; drunk eyes couldn't find me in the dark – up through the lungs. 'Do you think I care about your dad?' But Dad was already there, I think, Dad was standing by her – in through the belly – was it Dad?

'Do I know you?'

Fern hit me – up through the lungs – I remember her closing the gap between us with a hand flat and upraised – and back again out. She closed the gap and slapped the palm of her hand against my cheek and there was a slam in my ear and my head snapped and I was worried she'd drawn blood somehow because there was heat – up through the lungs. 'Jesus, what is the matter with you?' I was holding my face and she was laughing, was she? 'For those results you deserve it,' she said – in through the belly – in through the belly – in through the belly and I pushed the breath out in a rush as though it were stifling me. 'I won't let it drop, you know, I won't let you cheat, you little cheater,' she said and her hand was flat again – in through the belly – and I thought she was going to hit me so I moved and she tumbled but she didn't go on the floor – up through the lungs – but it made her angry all the same. 'You think you can pull the wool over me?' she said, and she was closer then, even though I was still backing away. 'Fern, please,' I started, but she laughed; a spiteful laugh like she hated me and I – in through the belly – didn't get a chance to finish before she said, 'I'll kill you, you stupid cow.' – up through the lungs – 'For making me look stupid like that. For making my results look bad. Don't think I won't! I'll kill you!'

And back again, out–

'Do I know you?'

SURPRISE

Humans have different levels of functioning including high, and barely.

I mixed up the social media campaigns for Pryke and Heafield. There was a flurry of angry and avid fans demanding to know the correct publication dates for each. The announcements had been inverted and there was no way of me catching the criticisms before they reached the ears of–

'Christ's sake, M, were you just not paying attention?' Eleanor talked down to me, figuratively and literally as she cornered me at my desk. 'Heafield is flipping her lid over this and I can't blame her. The book isn't out for another week and now all of the bloody excitement is premature and...' she petered out and dropped a heavy sigh. 'I thought we'd got past all this nonsense?'

I couldn't work out what nonsense she was referring to. 'Eleanor, look, I'm really sorry. I'll amend the dates across the remaining posts, and I'll write up an apology–'

'I'll write up the apology.'

'Okay, you can write up an apology and I'll post it at

lunchtime to get the midday traffic.' When she didn't respond I added, 'Is there anything else I can do about this?'

She crouched into my eyeline and lowered her voice to a whisper. 'You can drop the tone, or this cock-up will get all the way to Gladis.'

It seemed likely that it would make it all the way to Gladis either way, given that it was one of many cock-ups I'd managed to make in the two days since my memory homework had happened. Despite my best efforts I couldn't outrun Fern's criticisms. Or the stranger who – with some irony – was asking whether they knew me. I'd thought of enlisting the help of Mum again, to ask whether Fern and I had been close, whether she could tell me more than she had last time. But I'd let another three calls go unanswered in two days, and I didn't have the courage to face whatever fire was waiting.

An email appeared in the corner of my screen; marked *'Urgent'* from Eleanor. It was the promised apology and given the speed at which she'd sent it to me, I wondered whether she'd had a template ready – just waiting for a balls-up at my end. At last I'd given her cause to use it; she must have garnered a sick comfort from that.

After scheduling and rescheduling my mistakes, I took a good glance around the office to see how hard others were working. While they peered into each other's cubicles and loitered at the coffee-ing hole, I clicked into a browser and called up the news reports for the morning. There had been a handful of people in and out of Caleb's apartment, and there were occasions, too, where the woman without uniform came back but with Tuesday in tow. They would look around the apartment together and I wondered whether they were hunting for clues; I imagined them as a beautiful duo from a *Scooby Doo* episode which didn't feel right somehow. Their demeanours from a distance didn't give too much away – and neither did the news. The search was ongoing. *'It just isn't like him to disappear like this,'* an unnamed friend had said and I wondered whether it was The Redhead...

On the walk home from work I called Isaac's office to ask whether he could bring my appointment forward. I considered asking whether he could see me at the end of his workday but that seemed a stretch. An automated voice cut my plans short though – 'If you'd like to speak to one of our counsellors, please leave your name, number, and the name of the counsellor you're trying to reach.' – so I reasoned the only thing I could do was to try the memory exercise, again. I'd built the process into a conjuring, as though Fern's ghost might reach through the time between us and give me something other than profanities and threats. But the more she shouted the easier it was to understand how the memory had been misplaced.

I bargained with myself that if I made one more good attempt, I could take a Saturday morning walk past Caleb's building – from idle curiosity, I lied (to myself, though, so it hardly counted as a lie at all). With a strong resolve to have dinner and unpleasant memories on my Friday evening agenda, I stepped out of the lift in my building but walked straight into–

'Mum.'

'Surprise.' She flashed a tight smile. 'You weren't answering.'

'There's a reason for that,' I replied, fumbling for my keys. 'Now isn't a good time.'

'Okay, love. When is?'

She flashed the same tight smile and I let out a near-grunt. 'Christ, come on then, I can afford you a cup of tea.' I tried to lighten my tone but I sounded brittle, tired. 'Do you even want tea, or coffee, squash instead?' I made my attempts at hosting while I walked along the hallway to the kitchen, discarding my workbag on the floor as I went.

'I'll put the kettle on. You look like you need it more than I do.' She busied herself with water and mugs, and I couldn't find the energy to intervene. I closed my eyes and leaned back against the nearest cupboard. 'Are you still obsessing over this whole thing?'

I sighed and looked at her. I'd assumed it was a reference to her illicit affair with Dad. But she was holding the Fern Norton book, inspecting the front cover and then the back.

'I suppose so. I'm struggling with counselling at the minute. It's got me thinking – were she and I close, would you say?'

Mum shook her head. 'Not close, but there was a big group of you.'

'Did she ever come to the house?'

'Not that I can think of, love. Why do you ask?'

I laughed. 'I have a kind of, I don't know, near-memory of her being there.'

'Maybe she came over when I was out? Who's to say.' She set the book down and grabbed milk from the fridge, turning back to the task in hand. 'It was a long time ago, though, love, I wouldn't go worrying about those things now.' She turned and handed me my favourite mug, steaming with near-black tea. 'Did you try looking through the things I brought over?'

'There was a scrapbook.' But the thought of finding something in those memories was becoming as worrying as never finding them at all. 'I don't really know that it'll help.'

'It can't hurt to try.' She sipped her drink. 'It might shake something loose at least.'

'That's true,' I agreed. And while that could have been a good thing, it was still also the thing I was afraid of.

MEMORIES

There are times when the future should also be left in the past.

The memories I hadn't placed yet were things I was already looking forward to letting go of. Having had no luck in tracing one unaccounted for human, I thought I'd try my luck with another and switch my attentions back to Fern. But I couldn't bring myself to spend another chunk of time listening for those godforsaken spheres to smash together, all the while wondering whether I was missing something important in the living room opposite my own. At least in the bedroom the only view was of surrounding buildings packed with people who didn't interest me. I stood a better chance of concentrating, I reasoned, which might mean a better chance of finding something.

All the paraphernalia that Mum had brought over had been sitting in the bottom of my cupboard for weeks. I'd stuffed everything back into the bag it had arrived in and stashed it out of eyesight. It was further towards the back than I'd realised, and I had to shift a gym kitbag out of the way to get to it. How long it had been since I'd even ventured to a gym, I couldn't say. From the lip of the holdall there was a grey hoodie peering out, and a stray lace from a trainer, but they were things I hardly recognised. I pushed it to one side to clear space for the treasure I'd been searching for; the scrapbook was wedged awkwardly on top of everything else in the bag, like a lid to a memory box. I thought of making it a lucky dip; exercising some childhood innocence and delving a hand in to see what I might be lucky enough to bring out.

I pulled in a big breath and delved in with my eyes tightly closed, as though I might dictate the outcome. The disposable camera was the first thing I found; clunky and awkward and outdated. I wound up the mechanism on the side and heard that the film was full. The most logical thing would be to get it developed; reservations aside. I threw it, aiming for the bed, so it would be a safe distance away from the bag. It lowered the risk that I might accidentally-on-purpose pack it away again at the end of this exercise.

There was all sorts of crap to be found in the rest of the bag: an envelope of cinema tickets from films I couldn't remember the plots of; pressed petals, that I couldn't remember the significance of; a troll with wild hair that should have been attached to a pencil. Under other circumstances, taking a walk down the memory lane of adolescence wouldn't have been the worst thing – but the whole process felt tainted. With everything that I removed from the bag, I paused for inspection and interrogation; why might I have kept this, I asked, what might this mean. The reality being that I kept things for the same reasons most people do; we like to have things to hold on to. The bag was evidence of that if nothing else.

When nothing else lit a fire of memories around me, I tried the scrapbook again. Mum had been right when she said there was a big group of us; you had to go through several pictures sometimes to find the same face twice. But in every picture we looked happy. It was a documentation of hideous haircuts on my part; everything from when I thought growing it out into a long ponytail would be the coolest thing, right up to cutting it all off and starting with a fresh head of cropped hair. Fern and I weren't pictured standing together, but there were pictures of us throughout – buffered by a ram of people between us when we were all testing how many people you could fit inside a picture frame. I wondered whether the camera would add to this collection, once I'd got it developed.

'What happened to you?' I tapped my index finger along Fern's face, blocking out the childhood friend next to her. 'Why can't I find you?'

Although having the memories lying around was an unwelcome reminder of the things I'd mentally misplaced, I decided to leave the scrapbook to one side – where I'd stumble across it again easily. It couldn't hurt too much to have the occasional glance, in the hope that one day, one picture at least might be a trigger.

Further into the bag I found a sleeve, marked up as containing photographs. The only images in there, though, were ones of me and Dad. They were a display of childhood happiness and teenage reluctance, as my expressions moved through delighted-to-be-there and do-we-really-need-a-photo. The very last one from the bunch showed a different kind of animosity though. It was hard to place my age when I couldn't place the memory, but I guessed at sixteen or seventeen – from my rugged jeans and oversized Nirvana sweatshirt too. Dad had his arm around my shoulder and he was wearing his best fake smile; which Mum never noticed, but I clocked at a young age. I, however, was making no effort to smile at all in the picture. It wasn't reluctance; it was – something closer to disgust.

'Are you going to tell?' I could hear him saying, clear as a bell. But I didn't know when.

I filed the Father-and-Teen pictures back into their envelope and set them out of reach. My bedroom floor looked as though someone had emptied my teenage years onto the hard wood and I felt a tug of sadness. *Everyone must feel like this*, I reasoned, but I wasn't entirely convinced that everyone did. It had been an hour and forty minutes since I'd started to inspect these artefacts and I decided that one last dip into the bag would do – I'd made a decent enough effort, which I'd be able to tell Isaac at least.

The last item was cool – smooth. I didn't recognise it by touch so I pulled it out for closer inspection. It was a phone. When I clicked the home screen nothing happened; there was either no battery or the handset had been turned off. I turned it this way and that as though looking for a secret message, inscribed somewhere that might explain the find. The Apple logo looked brightened when the light from the window hit it. I decided against finding a charger, or even trying to turn the thing on. I clenched my hand around it and reached back into the bag, burying it as low down as I possibly could. When I felt a stir of nerves somewhere between my belly and my throat, I wondered whether I might misplace the knowledge of having found the phone at all. An iPhone XS, I guessed at. Something too new to belong to an old memory.

EVIDENCE

There's no such thing as damning evidence – if you're quick enough.

In the early hours of the morning I dug through the guts of my wardrobe to the bag of memories and pulled out the phone. I couldn't stand knowing it was there but doing nothing with it. Eventually I decided to stash it under the pillow on the opposite side of the bed; close enough but not touching, as though I might contaminate myself somehow – as though I hadn't already. I slept fitfully, reaching out often to touch the cold back of the handset. There was a point when, half-asleep, I flirted with the idea of pressing the on button; I wondered what I might find, whether a picture of Caleb and Tuesday would flash up as the lock screen. Then what would happen? Every time I arrived at that point in the imagining, I hit the brakes on it and tried to fall back into sleep – but even there there wasn't rest.

The morning light came in slowly through my living-room window; the sunshine an intruder on the city somehow, on what should have been a grim September morning. I waited for the first hours of the day to tick by, perched on my sofa at an angle that afforded me a view of the window. Despite my many searches, I hadn't been able to find a news report that mentioned anything about a missing phone. Not that I knew what I'd do with that information even if I had it; arrive at the police station waving the handset around? 'Coo-ee!' I might shout. 'I've got something you don't have.' In the kitchen I made more coffee and pushed the thought away; it didn't seem like an idea that would help things.

After the third cup of coffee it was a sociable enough hour to get dressed and face the world. The doorways of shops were yawning open and early birds were filtering in slowly; this was the quietest time on any given day in a city like Birmingham. I was grateful for the Friday-night drinkers, hardly awake at home still, while I was hurrying into Boots like someone on the run – an analogy I shook away quickly.

'Good morning, how can I help you?' The woman at the photo desk was overly chirpy. Her smile was coat-hanger wide, outlined by thick lip liner as though she wanted to draw attention to her mouth. I was conscious of staring while I answered.

'I have a camera film that I want developed.' I dropped the old Kodak on the counter, and it landed with a clumsy noise.

'You've come to the right place.' She laughed and picked up the camera. *Good*, I thought, *now there's someone else's fingerprints on it*. Although I didn't know why that caused me such relief; I should have handed her the phone instead. 'This is quite an old camera by the looks of things. We'll have a go at developing the film but there's a chance the images might not be entirely clear.' She paused as though expecting me to say something and when I didn't she added, 'Is that okay?'

'Sorry, Saturday morning brain.' I forced a laugh. 'Absolutely, whatever you can do.'

'Can you come back in,' she checked her watch, 'around an hour? Ten-ish?'

'No problem.'

From the upstairs photo desk to the downstairs doors I felt my heart knock against my ribs in irregular beats. There was the sudden panic of what might be on the camera to contend with, given that young-me hadn't thought to do it before. But maybe I'd forgotten the camera even existed. If recent events were anything to go by, then...

When I left the shop I found myself gulping in air. I was suddenly grateful for the godawful stench of inner-city pollution, and I decided to let it linger around me for an hour. There was nothing I needed from town, so I walked – and watched. People around me were starting to hurry, as though they were somehow already late for whatever lay ahead of them. When I started to walk through small clusters of loud teenagers and excited shoppers I realised I'd made a wrong turn somewhere, and I aimed myself at a quieter path.

The canal stretch was more of a through-line, taking people to other places, rather than a destination itself. I paced along and checked my watch every few minutes; there was still so much time to kill, and my own company was – either too much or too little, I couldn't decide. I found a bench to settle on and pulled my phone out. Mum's phone number was the last in my call records – which was a relief, given recent finds – so I tapped the green icon to call her. I should make the effort, I'd decided, at some point during the early hours. But three rings in I wondered whether I'd made a move too soon.

There was a long pause when the call connected, and then, 'She's just coming, kid, hang on.' The line went muffled. 'Hurry up, you can do that after.'

I disconnected the call. Knowing that it was happening was one thing, knowing when was another. Mum called back seconds later but I didn't answer; the moment had passed for a

Saturday morning confessional so I decided to sit quietly with my worries until I could go back and collect the photographs.

In my left-hand pocket was the phone – not my phone, but the other phone. I'd brought it with me, as though keeping it on my person were somehow safer. While I pressed my thumb hard against the home screen, I thought that maybe home would have been a safer place for it after all. There's nothing like being caught with evidence on your person; you saw it in documentaries all the time. If the evidence was found elsewhere there was always the chance that you could deny it – say you didn't know how it got there.

'Which would actually be the truth,' I said aloud but under my breath. I made a tight O-shape with my lips and forced out a steady stream of air. The same thrum of my heart rate was happening again; the same twist of nerves in my stomach. Mum called again while I tried to practise breathing and I resisted the urge to throw my phone into the water. It wouldn't fix anything, I reasoned. But the water was tempting.

Old and muddied from years of misuse. My reflection was a grim picture when I looked into the basin. I'd hardly slept, and it wouldn't take a genius to spot the signs of it. The phone was cold against my fingers and I wrapped my hand around it, pressing it hard into my palm as though I were trying to warm the thing. *It's dangerous*, I thought, *it's dangerous to have this and do nothing with it*. Then my own phone buzzed again, sending a jump of surprise through me.

'Guilty conscience,' a voice asked. I turned to look at the culprit and saw an older man nearby who I didn't recognise. He smiled. 'Something my grandmother used to say,' he explained. 'When you see someone jump, they might have a guilty conscience.'

I tried to force a laugh. 'That sounds like old wisdom.'

'Probably. She wasn't often wrong though, my grandmother.'

He moved to carry on walking. 'Either way, be careful jumping around that close to the edge. You wouldn't want to tumble in; they'd never find you in that muck.'

Wouldn't I? The thought came like a knee-jerk reaction. I watched him walk away – less from interest and more to make sure he'd gone. There were few passers-by, but no one who looked distracted enough to pay attention to me. I grabbed the phone between my thumb and index finger inside my pocket and, as I turned to have another hard look at my surroundings, I dropped the handset. It landed in the water with a loud plop that I thought might draw attention, and yet no one said a word – no one shouted out, either, as I started to walk away. On the stretch of time back to collect my photographs I wondered whether I could convince myself I'd dropped the phone by accident – or whether, somehow, covering up for myself was second nature.

HER

Things often come to us when we stop looking for them.

There was nothing incriminating on the photographs. The pictures were muddied and faded in some places, from the years spent trapped inside the camera. But mostly they were happy pictures of me with friends – and Fern. In some shots there was the campfire that I'd managed to place from a memory, and I wondered whether the images might turn out to be a gift; photo evidence of the night that time forgot. After I'd skimmed through them, to check there really was nothing to panic about, I took them home and spread them out across the living-room floor. Every few images, there was a shot of Fern – smiling, staring, sometimes blurring as she tried to prop herself next to someone else in the picture. Her eyes were black and blank, how I'd remembered them being. I flitted between shots but spent time with each, allowing for a few minutes to pass as though a memory might come naturally – without tweezers and a spotlight to pry it out. After two hours I began to feel like I was holding a séance – which I suppose in some ways I was. And eventually the dead girl came through.

One of the images was Fern by herself. Her face was pulled

into a grimace that only drunk people can make, and I imagined her cussing at whoever was behind the camera – me? There was no way to know but it seemed likely, from the things I'd remembered. There came another wave, then, like before, while I stared at that expression; something that washed over me all at once as though it had always been there, on the verge.

'How did you manage it? You're thick as shit at the best of times.'

'You'll wake my dad.'

'Who cares about your dad?'

I took a deep breath in – through the belly up through the lungs and back again – out and focused on the picture.

'I could beat you any day of the week, at anything.'

In through the belly up – Fern stumbled around the garden, unsteady on her feet. She moved her mouth but there weren't sounds coming out and I wondered whether I'd misplaced the dialogue – through the lungs and back – but she was definitely saying – 'Are you listening to me, stupid? Stupid, stupid...' – she sounded full of venom – again – out – in–

I lost track of my breathing and the memory went with it but there was something left behind – like a residue. Fern had followed me home. We were at the campfire together and I left and then she–

'You can't tell me what to do!' she shouted. I breathed in – through the belly up – to steady myself but it was then and before all at once. 'Are you listening?' she asked, and I turned to face her because I'd been looking at the house – up – waiting for a bedroom light to snap on. 'We'll wake my dad,' I kept saying and she – through the lungs and back again – 'Do you think I care about your dad? I care about you! You and your perfect results!' – in through the belly – and she was angry because it was results day and I'd done better than everyone expected of me, because – 'Everyone knows you're stupid, so how'd you–' –

up through the lungs – 'What the bloody hell is this nonsense?' Dad asked, pushing the back door open with a clatter and I told him Fern was leaving and she said she wasn't. 'I want answers,' she shouted, even at Dad and I remember his surprise, that a young girl might shout like that. 'Whatever this is can be fixed in the morning when you've sobered up,' he told her and she laughed – actually laughed in a vicious and spiteful and – back again out, and in– 'You're not my father!' she shouted and he was shouting back then. 'It's a bloody good job too, Fern Norton, because I'd be sorely disappointed.'

My breath caught somewhere in the back of my throat and I tumbled forwards. When my hands reached out to stop myself they caught the pictures, scattering them everywhere. But touching them made it all the more tangible as though the memory were a physical thing. I took a deep breath in – through the belly up – and panted on all fours, like a wild thing birthing something – through the lungs and back again–

'I will kill her for what she's done!' she shouted, and I really believed her. She closed the gap between us; she was unsteady but made quick progress. I moved away – in through the belly – but I knew that she was going to hit me again, I felt certain of a second slap which meant the first must have already happened. 'Fern, don't make me...' – through the lungs and back again – '... I really don't want – Fern, please,' I said over and over and I couldn't see Dad anymore and–

'You need to stop crying, kid, okay?' Dad said, but we weren't at home anymore. I didn't recognise the surroundings. It was dark and it might have been a different evening, but no, it couldn't have been because–

The vibration of my mobile against hard wood pulled me back, as though the whole thing were only a mirage. I grabbed the handset, hoping it might be Mum again because I felt like I needed another human, but it wasn't a phone call. In the hours of not sleeping I'd set up a search engine alert for Caleb's name, having decided that the constant refreshing of browser pages was too much like waiting for *The X Factor* results. There were four different articles lined up on the screen announcing that an official statement had been made first thing. I clicked the first of the links and sucked a breath in while it loaded. The anticipation was too much for me to read everything in detail but I skimmed – in through the belly up through the lungs and back again out – and practised breathing while the best and worst words jumped out at me. *'Officially a missing person'* they were calling him, *'suspicious disappearance'* that was *'very out of character'*. The police were searching for Caleb and a number of his personal effects including *'his mobile phone, which hasn't been used since August 6th'* and items of clothing including *'the shirt Mr Neale is pictured wearing here'* along with his *'gym bag, containing...'*

I didn't read on, though. Because I already knew what was in the bag.

PART V

ME

It seems strange to confess to something – even though I'm an honest person.

There's no statute of limitations in the United Kingdom and I know this because I've googled it, on four separate occasions, since remembering what happened the night Fern Norton died. I've also cross-referenced my initial findings with seven different websites in total and, because I'm not an idiot, I used Wendy's computer at work to do this.

I've never done anything like this before – which sounds like something I'd say to the police. It's definitely something I've said to lovers, friends, and my parents once or twice.

'I've never done anything like this before,' I told Mum when she caught me bunking off school. It had been four days since Fern's body had been found – the start of a new term and everything – and I couldn't stand to be around the collective grief of everyone in our year – never mind the spill-out from it that had somehow managed to contaminate the rest of the school.

'So why are you doing it now?' she asked.

'It's hard at school at the minute.'

'Because of Fern?'

I shuddered when I heard her name. 'I guess.'

'Love,' she lowered herself into my eyeline, 'you can't just bunk off like that. And to hang about in the woods as well? After some – after some bloody animal left Fern there.'

'She's right, kid,' Dad chimed in. He gave me a knowing look and a raised eyebrow from behind Mum's back. 'You've got to keep yourself together in times like these.'

'You're allowed to grieve, of course,' Mum added.

'But in an orderly fashion?' I stood up. 'I'd like to go to my room now.'

'Tough,' Dad said, setting a hand on my shoulder to sit me back down. 'What happened to Fern was something dreadful and terrible, but you can't let it ruin your life like this, not when you're doing so well at everything.'

'We understand, love, that she was a friend, and this must be a scary time.'

The two alternated between soft and hard edges. I preferred Mum's style of kindness.

'It's hard, walking around and knowing what happened,' I said but I spoke more to Dad than I did to Mum. 'I know it must be hard for everyone. But, knowing...'

'Kid,' Dad sat down next to me, 'do you want this to ruin your life?' When I didn't answer he placed a finger under my chin and guided my eyeline towards him. 'Listen to me, do you want this to ruin everything you've worked for?'

'No,' I answered, flatly. 'No, of course not.'

'Grieve, but go to school. It's important that we start putting this behind us.'

That was the end of their lecture. We spent the rest of the evening pretending to be a normal family; we even shared a meal, which we hadn't done in – I couldn't remember how long. Mum let me choose the television programme we watched for after dinner but, during the wait for it, the evening news splashed across the screen – announcing and re-announcing Fern's death, for anyone who'd been living under a stone.

'Terrible, isn't it,' Mum said.

'Dreadful,' Dad replied.

And I wondered how he did it – acted normal. All the while knowing everything.

WORK

Consider how people might describe you if they were questioned.

People who didn't have a jot of knowledge about Caleb and his life were suddenly professional experts in how he lived. There had been television reports and shared Facebook posts, Instagram stories and watering hole gossip, where I loitered and listened to colleagues decide what a brilliant man he must have been – all because he looked good on a high definition television screen. While days rolled by I tried to fall into something like autopilot, to keep myself going. But it was impossible to ignore their chatter.

'He was a good-looking chap, wasn't he?'

'The girlfriend is beautiful.'

'I heard he was quite an up and comer.'

I bit back on correcting them. She wasn't his girlfriend. And it didn't escape my attention that despite there not being proof of death, people had already decided on it. Everything was said in the past tense – which didn't make my denial of it all any easier.

After hearing more rumour-mill gossip about him, I decided

to put in a holiday request. In the entire time I'd worked at the company I'd never taken my allotted leave; where would I have gone? Now, however, I wanted to go home and stay there for as long as I could, with minimal commentaries on Caleb's whereabouts – if they could be avoided. But I knew I'd google them all the same, whether I had colleagues to fill the role or not.

The holiday request hadn't been as easy as I'd thought, though, with an instant message from Gladis asking that I pop along to her office when I had the time. I thought of telling her I didn't have the time at all, but it hardly seemed like it would support my ploy to leave for two weeks if I used 'being busy' as an excuse to avoid her.

The door was ajar enough for her to see me on my approach and, with her desk phone still pressed to her ear, she waved me in.

'I know, yes... Yes, Stephen, I... Yes, I know that.' She rolled her eyes at me and mouthed, 'Sorry.' I smiled. 'I'm with one of our social media managers now... Yes, right in front of me... Of course.' She slammed the phone down without a formal goodbye. 'Good Lord.' She laughed. 'Stephen Ward. Have you met him?'

'I can't place the name.'

'Author turned agent. He's making a nuisance of himself with one book or a – oh, do you know, that isn't why I asked you to come in.' She sniffed. 'M, apologies.'

'I thought you said...' I trailed off and gestured to her phone.

'Oh, only to get him off the phone,' she explained. 'I wanted to talk through holiday.'

'I'm sure I have the time available. I haven't taken any breaks so far this year.'

'I know, and you're owed one.' I could hear the 'but' coming from a clear mile away. 'But it's hardly the best timing, is it? The

Sell and Wilkinson publications are set to be big, big events in our calendar this year and we could really do with someone of your experience on hand to deal with those releases. Do you see?'

'I do, but there's a whole team available for that. I can brief them before I go–'

'You're the best we have, though, M.'

It was the first compliment I'd been paid since my very first day on the job, when Eleanor had told me she liked my workbag. 'That's kind of you to say but–'

'Oh, you dear.' She tilted her head and flashed me a sympathetic look. 'You really do need the break, don't you?'

I didn't know what I'd done to trigger the change. But I blindly agreed. 'Yes, really.'

'A full two weeks?'

Admittedly, two weeks with immediate effect had been a bold request on my part and I'd expected some reluctance to it. Which is why I knew that I'd potentially need something to soften the blow with – and what better than the truth?

'Honestly, Gladis, the reason I need a break, and at such short notice, is for mental health reasons.' The confession came naturally; in fact, there was a small tug of relief at having shared the truth with someone. 'I've lost a friend recently,' also true, I told myself as I tried to steady my breathing, 'and I'm having a hard time coming to terms with all of the changes around that. I realise it's not perfect timing, and I apologise–' She held up a hand to pause me. I wasn't keen on the increasing amount of interruptions.

'There's no need to explain any further. You're more than entitled to compassionate leave, don't go using your holiday for something like that. Will the two weeks be enough?'

I let out a surprised, 'I should think so.'

'Does that cover the funeral time?' she asked in a deliberately soft tone.

'I'm sorry?'

'The funeral for your friend. You said – you said you'd lost?'

More like misplaced, I thought. 'Oh, I'm sorry. Yes, yes it covers the funeral.'

'Okay, M, well, whatever you need. Are you okay to stay for the rest of the day, to make sure everything's in order before your break?'

'Of course, that won't be a problem.' I stood. 'I really appreciate you being so understanding, Gladis. It's a difficult time.'

She reached across her desk to grab my hand. 'I know what you're going through.' She gave me a light squeeze and I wondered whether she really did – although it seemed unlikely.

The concern came somewhere on my walk back to my desk. *Would this be used against me at a later date?* I wondered whether the police would ask my colleagues what they thought of me – whether there were any standout incidents worth commenting on. *Might they use this as evidence?* I wondered, sitting back down at my desk. *Would they ask whether my behaviour was at all suspicious?* I half-laughed as I keyed in my password and restarted work. *Suspicious behaviour*, I thought again; would my colleagues even have been able to tell?

THERAPY

I f at first you don't remember – ask the same question again.

There was a comfortable silence between me and Isaac. But after five minutes had ticked by on the clock with neither of us saying anything, I started to worry that this might go on forever if neither of us cracked.

'Is there something I'm meant to be talking about?' I asked.

'You looked like there was something you were waiting to talk about.'

I shook my head; I didn't understand how he could have known that from my expression, and I wondered what else I might be giving away. 'It's been a difficult few days,' I admitted. 'I tried the memory recall exercise again. Actually,' I rubbed at the side of my aching forehead, 'I've tried it a few times.' It had become a nightly ritual, but I didn't want to admit to that for fear of giving something else away.

'Would you say it's been successful?'

'In some ways.' I hadn't been able to place what had happened to Caleb. But I had remembered washing my hands; mud on boots; cleaning the laminate of the hallway. 'I think I have a full memory.'

'Okay,' he edged forward in his seat, 'can you breathe with me for a second?'

I hadn't realised that my chest's rise and fall had increased, become erratic even. I watched Isaac and copied his in- and exhales until my own felt steadier.

'I'm sorry.'

'There's really no need to be.' He sat back. 'Memory recall can be traumatic for lots of reasons. We're digging around in places that our brain doesn't want us to go, so it's only natural that it might cause some panic.' He smiled and I tried to reciprocate but it felt more like I was grimacing. 'Do you want to talk me through the memory?'

I shook my head again. 'I don't think I do.'

'How about the feelings around it?'

'Disappointment,' I said, before I really had time to consider it.

'In the memory?'

'I think so.' The different scenes flitted in front of my eyes, like a film I could remember the plot to, but not necessarily the order of things happening. 'Disappointment that I worked so hard to find something I now don't want.'

'Because it's a bad memory?'

I laughed. 'I don't know what else I was expecting.'

'We knew that remembering things could bring up something unpleasant, right? Your brain is blocking out things that it doesn't want to keep a hold of. So, if we're trying super hard to remember those things, it's likely that we'll find some badness there. But forcing ourselves to remember and process and work through these things properly can lead to a lot of goodness.' He spoke slowly, as though dealing with a child; there was something more comforting about that than usual.

'How accurate are memories?' He sighed, and I looked up in

time to catch the expression that went with it. 'We already talked about this,' I said, as though filling in a blank.

'A few times now.' He let a beat of silence pass between us. 'There are mixed memories floating around in our brains because sometimes we remember things, and sometimes we remember the memory of it. Does that sound familiar?'

I thought – hard. I imagined rifling through the detritus and dead leaves in the back of my brain somewhere until I found what felt like an educated guess. 'Internal and external?'

He smiled. 'Exactly.'

There was a sense of accomplishment somewhere in my gut at having remembered. 'I wish I could recall other things as quickly.'

'We'll get there. For now, let's think a little more about this full memory.'

'I said I didn't want to–'

'You don't have to tell me what it is,' he interrupted. 'Let's think about who it involves.'

I tried to choose my words carefully. 'The girl is there. The one who died.'

'Is it the campfire memory?'

'It starts that way. But Dad is there, too, by the end of it.'

'Have you spoken to him about this memory?'

I felt my eyes widen at the very suggestion. 'I haven't – I mean, I've wanted – it's felt too soon,' I eventually said, shaking away my false starts. 'I haven't worked out what to say yet.'

It had surprised me that he and I had managed to keep the secret all these years. Less me, maybe, because no sooner had I made the memory and I misplaced it again. The awkward days and weeks that followed Fern's death had come flooding back along with the memories of losing her. But he'd always known. And since learning that, I wondered what Mum had been privy to over the years. In the memory he's shouting; he's asking whether I'll tell her, whether I can keep this to myself and–

Isaac set a hand on my knee. 'Are you still with me?'

'I'm sorry.' I shook my head, but the memory wouldn't leave now I'd found it.

'I realise that talking to your father might be difficult, especially if it's a memory that you're not comfortable sharing. But if he understands that this is something to help you, to help with your lapses, surely he'd want to assist in some way?'

I nodded along – but I didn't know that I agreed. 'I've wondered whether Mum knows.'

'She was there?'

'No, no I don't know where she was. But they might have talked.'

'In my experience, families who are in touch will always try to find ways to help recovery.' He flashed a smile. 'You might surprise yourself if you have a sit-down conversation with them, one at a time even, you don't have to rush everything all at once. But there's a possibility that they'll be more ready for this talk than you might think.'

I smiled, as though in agreement. But then I thought of Dad and his doting fiancée; the wedding that he'd be paying for well into his seventies, all for the sake of settling down afresh with someone – albeit someone he was already cheating on. Still, it didn't seem likely that he'd chance letting it all slip. But then I thought of Mum and her newly furnished apartment; how she'd downsized from the family home because what was the point in keeping a place that size all to yourself? She'd be the best starting point, I decided. Because she didn't have anyone to lose apart from me.

HIM

Self-care is about giving yourself exactly what you need sometimes.

The appointment with Isaac had been one of the most difficult I'd had. Which is why on the walk home I felt like I could justify treating myself. I called Mum to ask whether we could have dinner this week; when she didn't answer I left a voicemail where I tried to sound neutral and unaffected – as though I weren't about to accuse her of something heinous. By the time I was hanging up I was nearly at Caleb's building.

There was no one to ask about Caleb; no one I could borrow memories from or look through photographs with. I'd held and sniffed and slept with the gym-wear I'd found but it hadn't brought anything back. I had to believe that a walk by his block of flats might.

Dotted along the street, as though trying to make themselves blend into the surroundings, there were journalists. Some of them made a show of their camera crews and their flashy attire; standing, microphone in hand, to announce that there were no further updates. Some of them tried hard to blend into the background, by drinking coffee from window seats and doodling on the notebooks that they hoped would soon be rammed to bursting with details of Caleb's life. I bought myself a takeaway coffee and watched them all; I saw them come and go and come back again in the forty minutes that I was there.

After I'd waited for another twenty minutes, and seen another huddle of journalists give up their endeavour, I trod closer to the entranceway. I didn't have a splay of images to adorn my living-room floor with. But I reasoned that there might be something – the shadow of his doorway; the gate I must have pushed through; the sign that read '*Broken buzzer*' next to the intercom system – that would bring something back.

'Can I help you?' someone asked.

When I turned to see the source, I came face to face with a police officer. Her hair was scraped back into a bun, lowered enough to accommodate her hat. She was wearing black body armour and her shirt had the same crispness I'd seen on other officers walking through Caleb's home. I wondered whether she was here to stand guard.

'I'm sorry,' I said, trying to sound more flustered than I was. 'I was just...'

'Journalist?' she said, her eyebrow raised.

'No,' I half-laughed, 'no, not at all.'

'Oh,' she said, as though realising something. 'Are you...' she trailed off and narrowed her eyes at me. 'You're not – sorry, are you?' She sighed. 'Are you the partner?'

I smiled. 'No, not me.'

I guessed The Partner must be Tuesday's new name; sometimes dropped to The Girlfriend, depending on the knowledge of the speaker. She'd been referred to by so many different names since Caleb went missing, but she appeared – by any other name – still a rose in every picture publicly displayed. She looked beautiful in her anguish; meaning, she wore it much better than I could. But I supposed that she had reason to.

'Are you from the building?' She sounded suspicious; as though having exhausted the most obvious options, I must be a kind of leech looking for gossip.

I lowered my voice. 'Me and him, we were seeing each other, a little.' Her face didn't register surprise. If anything, I thought I saw the flicker of a smirk. 'It wasn't really common knowledge,' I tried to sound coy, 'and Louise, she didn't – doesn't know, even now.' Using the first name familiarity gave the grey lie that extra touch of believability and the woman shot me a look that made me think this was a situation she recognised.

'You're one of the girlfriends.'

It wasn't a question, but I agreed all the same. 'One of.'

'You've talked to DS Checkley, I assume?'

It was the first time I'd heard her name; the woman who changed the room whenever she walked into it. 'I've made myself known to her.'

'I'm sorry for your...' she petered out, unsure of what to offer her condolences on.

'Thank you.' I nodded to the building in the background. 'I'm getting semi-regular updates. I know there's nothing you can give away, not really, but I'll just kick myself if I don't ask. Are they any closer to – God, I don't know. Do they even know what happened?'

She pressed her lips together. 'I'm afraid I can't–'

'Completely,' I interrupted her. 'Completely understandable.' I started to step back then, reasoning that if I left on good terms there would be even less of an excuse for her to remember me. 'Thank you for your help, all the same, and for your,' I took a deliberate pause and then shrugged, 'well, your understanding.'

'No trouble. You take care now.'

I carried on my way down the short walk between Caleb's building and mine. I always forgot how close we were until I trod the distance; for months we'd been only a three-minute walk away from each other. I buzzed myself in and took the lift to my floor, while my thoughts dashed between dinner and danger alert. Caleb was out there somewhere – one way or another – but it felt as though I couldn't stay fixed on the thought for long. Once my head was buried in the fridge, I stood even less chance of maintaining focus. But I wondered whether mindful meditation might be more conducive to accurate memory recall if I did it on a full stomach. So, I set the oven to pre-heat and went to wait in the living room until the timer was done for a ten-minute warm-up. During the in-between minutes I balanced myself against the window ledge and looked out onto the city; I watched nothing, though, and saw no one.

DINNER

When all else fails, bluff.

I had no idea how much Mum knew about the night of Fern Norton's death. While I made the journey from my home to hers, I tried on different versions of the evening to see whether that might help. In the memory she hadn't been there; but what if Dad had told her when she got home? What if – the reason he didn't want me to tell her was so he could spin a different story altogether? What if – what if – what if – I thought until I was standing outside her flat. Mum was an honest woman at heart, though, and it didn't matter how many versions of the lie or the truth I tried on, I couldn't see how she'd gone so long without mentioning Fern – if she knew. Similarly, even if Mum had been a liar, she certainly didn't have much of a game face. I'd brought Fern up in conversation more than once since I'd remembered her and everything that came with her. How had Mum kept her cool through that if she knew?

'I'm so glad you called about dinner,' she said as she opened the door, sidestepping a formal hello and going straight in for unashamed enthusiasm. I'd thought of inviting her over for dinner but the lure of my window-view had lost its pull, and at least eating at Mum's got me out of the house – something I was doing less, since taking my leave from work. 'I'm just making a little pasta dish. It's in the oven browning. I got a jump on with it, because I thought you'd be hungry from work.' The explanations rushed from her and I realised how nervous she must be. I felt the same; although I thought, all things considered, I had more reason to be.

'I'm not at work right now,' I answered, following her from living room to kitchen.

She snapped around. 'Is everything okay?'

'I just needed a break.'

'Love,' she closed the distance between us, 'is this because – of what you know?'

Yes, I thought. But that's not what she meant. 'Because of you and Dad?'

She placed a hand either side of my face as though trying to make sure my gaze stayed with her. 'It isn't, is it? Because of us?'

'No, Mum.' I pulled away. 'I'm just having a bit of a time of it at the minute.'

'Well, shall we talk about that?' She opened the oven door, releasing a ball of heat into the room that she waved away with a gloved hand. 'Yep, that's done.'

'Does the table need setting?' I asked, mostly to avoid her question.

'Already done.' She set the hot tray on a large serving board. 'You go and get settled. I'll just switch things off in here then I'll be in. Then maybe we can talk?' Her intonation suggested it was a question but I knew otherwise; it was a command.

I followed the first round of orders and went into the living room, where Mum's makeshift dining table was assembled. This was a far cry from the lengthy dining table that we spent my childhood around. Mum had only given the house up twelve months before; the empty spaces and stale memories had got to her in the end. Although, with memories afresh, I wondered what evidence she might have accidentally passed on to the new homeowners in having sold the place.

'There we go.' She set the serving tray down. 'Dig in,' she said, already serving me a too-big portion. She hummed away to herself while she spooned three great lumps of pasta onto my plate and then set about dishing up her own. I noted that she only had one scoop; Mum always lost her appetite when she was nervous. 'How are you feeling then, love? About things?'

'About you and Dad?'

She shrugged, as though she hadn't angled us towards this. 'Generally.'

'Mum–'

'I'm worried that you hate us,' she spat out, but her face fashioned an expression that suggested she regretted her phrasing. 'Not hate, that's too strong.'

'Are you still seeing each other?' I asked. But I deliberately didn't make eye contact. Instead I forked a heap of pasta into my mouth and waited out the silence. I looked up as I swallowed and clocked her twitch immediately; her left eye pulled down ever so slightly at the edge, a flicker every two to three seconds. 'That's a yes.'

'We haven't talked much.'

'No, he and I haven't either. There's stuff I need to talk to him about, though, so he'll have to talk to me at some point.' I took another mouthful and tried to remain casual; as though I hadn't just laid live bait on the table between us.

'Well, what do you need to talk to him about?'

Mum was a strong advocate in kids from divorced families having a relationship with both parents. But even when they'd been together she'd hated the thought of missing out on something – that there might be something Dad was better at.

Like teaching me how to set up a tent for the Duke of Edinburgh camping trips, for example, or disposing of a body.

'Fern,' I answered plainly, my mouth still half-full. 'There's some stuff that I'm working through with my counsellor and I think Dad might be able to help me understand it all.' I waited a good beat of silence – nearly a whole chew – before I looked up at her. 'You weren't there when it happened, were you?'

'The night it happened, you mean?' She didn't miss a beat in answering, and her tone didn't change. 'I was away with Madge and the book club girls.' Mum said 'book club' but meant 'drinking club' and there had been an unspoken agreement about that when I was younger. But she still didn't seem unsettled at the topic. 'He said that you'd got back fine, said you'd had enough of the campfire antics early on.' She frowned. 'Have you remembered something different?'

I hesitated over which version of events to share. 'A little different.' I swallowed another mouthful. 'If you weren't there then it really doesn't matter, Mum.'

She chewed and thought and swallowed. 'I can't remember him saying there'd been any trouble or anything at all, love, no. I'm sorry.' She forked her last two pieces of pasta. 'I suppose he would be best for something like that.' She sounded sad at the admission and I believed her reaction. But what Dad's reaction would be was something else.

'This is great, Mum, really.' I tried to shift the subject, eating the last of the scraps.

'You really don't hate us?' she asked again, with the sadness from before.

I half-laughed to try to break the tension. 'No, Mum, I really don't hate you. I think you both have terrible taste in partners,' I set my cutlery down, 'but who am I to talk?'

She laughed then and her relief was obvious. 'Pudding?'

'Please!' I laid on the enthusiasm. 'Need help?'

'Not even a little. You stay where you are.' She started to clear away. 'Let me look after you for an hour or two at least, now I've got you here. Do you fancy something warm or something...' she trailed off out of earshot as she walked into the kitchen.

While I half-listened to her clattering around in the next room, I pulled my phone out from my front pocket. There weren't any new updates about Caleb's case – which was both a blessing and not all at once. I pulled up a fresh message and thumbed down to my dad's number.

'Did you say hot or cold?' Mum asked, sticking her head back into the room.

'Hot, please.' I smiled. When she disappeared I finished typing.

'I know what really happened.'

And I hit send.

POLICE

Sometimes you have to make it impossible for people to ignore you.

Dad didn't reply to my first message; nor the messages I sent in the days afterwards. The first drafts of each text were increasingly erratic to the point that I had to carefully edit every message before I sent it – and he still didn't reply. None of the messages mentioned Fern by name, admittedly. But what else could I have been referring to? I considered a blunter approach – *'I know what happened when Fern died.'* – but I'd become more mindful of what might be used against me at a later date these days. There were still police traipsing in and out of Caleb's flat on a daily basis and a view like that will make you cautious about your own behaviours after a time. I took inspiration from my view once, though, typing a message to Dad – *'I'm going to the police about it.'* – that I thought really would light a fire. But it was too terrible to bluff about.

'Have you spoken to Dad at all?' In the end I brought in emergency services and called Mum. 'Like, since you saw me?' She hesitated in her answer so I added, 'I don't care what you were doing, I just wanted to know whether you'd seen him.'

'Once, but not for very long.'

I felt a grim shudder wash over me. 'Okay, thanks, Mum.'

When Mum had failed I called Carol.

'Oh, do you know something, dear, he's been saying for days that he needs to call you.'

'He has?' I didn't buy it. 'I guess he's just busy?'

'What with work and the wedding.' I'd called his work three times to get hold of him but every time he'd been out of the office. So there was a lie in the story somewhere. But Carol didn't seem to be the most likely source of it. 'He's in the office quite late tonight, I think, if you want to try to catch him there? But I can remind him again that he needs to call.'

'That would be great, Carol, if you wouldn't mind. Thanks.'

If he was in the office that day, he certainly wasn't answering his phone. I called another three times and left two messages. After such persistence on my part, when my front doorbell chimed a visitor later that evening, I'd assumed it would be him. I'd almost answered with a, 'Well it's about time', but felt glad that I hadn't gone quite that far when I saw who the guest actually was: The woman who changed a room when she walked into it.

'Hi there, I'm DS Lynda Checkley and this is my colleague DC Martin Grave. We were wondering whether we could have a quick chat with you?'

I flashed a tight smile. 'Of course.' I leaned hard against the doorway to signal a 'no entry'. *But does that look suspicious*, I wondered, so I corrected my stature and stood upright again. 'Did you want to come in?'

'If we could, that would be great.' She already had a foot across the boundary.

I stepped aside. 'Please. If you take the first door on the right, that's the living room.' Which was the room they'd be most interested in seeing, I guessed. 'Can I ask what this is about?' I followed them.

DS Checkley was already looking out through the window. But she had her eyes angled down onto the street. 'Caleb Neale.' She looked up at me then. 'You've likely heard bits and pieces about the case on the news already?'

'Oh, the missing guy?' I tried to sound aloof. 'He was from around here, right?'

'More than around here,' her gaze flicked back to the building opposite, 'he was practically a neighbour of yours.'

'We're canvassing your building,' the other detective chimed in, 'to see whether anyone was familiar with Caleb, or even whether you happened to notice anything suspicious happening on the night of August 6th.'

'You've got a great view into his living room,' Checkley said, still looking.

'I've got a great view into lots of living rooms. I hardly need a television.' I laughed but the sound didn't come out right, instead emerging like an awkward cluck. 'I'm sorry, I have to confess I don't spend all that much time watching the building opposite.'

Checkley turned around and smiled. 'We'd be more concerned if you did.'

'Were you here on the night in question?'

'I was, yes. It started out as a night in front of the TV but it ended up as a night in the bathroom, I'm afraid. Stomach bug seemed to kick in out of nowhere.' I flashed a tight smile. 'I had to call in sick for work the following day and everything.' I tried not to be distracted by Checkley, who I could see hovering out of the corner of my eye. There was something about the woman that made me want to watch her though.

Her male junior handed over a card. 'If you happen to remember anything, maybe you could give us a call? That will bring you straight through to me.'

'Anything at all would be helpful at this point,' Checkley added, 'even if it was something happening on the street, someone rushing to or from a vehicle, anything like that.'

'Of course.' I took the business card. 'If there's anything, I'll be sure to get in touch. I think – now I've started I'm not sure, but I think the building, this building I mean, it should have some security cameras fixed to the outer walls. It was kind of a selling point when I moved in, the safeness of the place.' *That's it*, I thought, *help them to find you why don't you?* In the face of interrogations we all make stupid decisions, I reasoned. But it paid off.

Checkley gave me a sympathetic sort of smile, as though she thought I might be an idiot – which was no bad thing. 'We've got the CCTV footage already. But thank you.' She looked to her partner who nodded. 'Right, we'll leave you to your day.'

'Thanks again,' the other said while he walked back along the hallway.

'You're welcome. I'll call, if – you know.'

So at least I knew they'd got the cameras. Now I'd just have to wait for them to watch.

MEMORIES

We find things when we stop looking for them.

My parents came with me to collect my GCSE results; none of us had especially high expectations. I hadn't been a dumb teenager. But in the months ahead of my exams I'd become complacent with cleverness. After years of people telling me I was smart and I'd be fine, I took them at face value by doing little to no work at all from the middle of year ten. The mock exams had thrown up worries but still – 'It'll come good in the end, and these mocks don't always give us accurate ideas on things.' – teachers had soothed me. My parents, though, had more outright concerns over those first results. They became convinced that I was destined to mess up the exams, no matter how hard I worked for them; petulant and childish, I resolved to prove them wrong by not working all that hard at all. But by the time I'd torn open the paper and burst into happy tears at the string of As and Bs in front of me, all those concerns looked to be long forgotten.

'You're thick as shit, how did you manage that?' Alison – an alleged comrade – had joked. But it had been a joke – unlike

Fern's reaction, which looked to be disappointment, shock and outrage that I'd outdone her.

'We're so proud of you, love,' Mum said, ushering me away from friends. I wonder now if, having seen Fern's reaction, I should have said something to her then rather than wait for things to boil over. But in retrospect there were several things I'd change about results night.

'Honestly, kid, you've done great here.' Dad patted me on the back. It was the first time in months that I'd seen a happy united front from them both.

'These results, God, they're so good. We must celebrate, we must.'

'Dinner out?'

'Tonight?' I snapped. 'But…'

'Oh, don't you worry, I've remembered even if he hasn't.' Mum shot Dad a look. 'They're all going out and not drinking.' She leaned heavy on 'not' and then winked at me. She'd already bought me two tall bottles of WKD.

'In that case, lunch?' Dad asked.

We had a meal like any other family then – not like one that had been arguing for months about revision and child support and who blamed who for which part of the marriage having broken down. They'd been a turbulent few months for us all. It was nice, though, to be normal for a while.

My friends and I had agreed to meet for campfire antics at around seven that evening. But, never one to be too early to anything, I arrived half an hour after the others. The fire was already going and people were stacking their boozy offers into a splay of chill boxes that were just outside the circle – something David's mum had kindly provided for the event. Some people were standing, mingling, others were seated on discarded tree stumps and large branches that made for natural benches. Fern was sitting, wrapped around a boy who I didn't recognise – just her latest, I guessed – she stayed there for most of the night. She'd had a blurry-eyed look already when I arrived, and I hadn't been keen to kick the ants' nest of her temper; I knew what she was like.

'Parents still skipping about your results?' Duncan nudged me.

'Christ, I think I am,' I laughed back with him, 'As and Bs, man. I don't even–'

'Hey, come on now, you've always been a smart arse,' Rachel interrupted me. 'You should be pleased, really. You deserve those results.'

From somewhere behind us there was a deep snort and we all turned to see the source: Fern had surfaced. 'Some of us actually tried really fucking hard, you know?'

'Fern, get out of it,' Rachel tried to diffuse things, 'you'll make up for it.'

'Yeah, we've got our A Levels to cock up yet.' Duncan tried for a joke, but Fern threw him a look that could have killed a grown man. 'All right, or not. We could shit ourselves over these results instead.'

Fern might have had an axe she wanted to grind with me, but it was obvious that she wasn't sober enough to take on three people at once. She skulked back to the boy she'd left waiting and they stayed together through most of the evening. By the time I left, nearly everyone had coupled off into huddles that I thought they'd regret the following day. But I never had been one to make romantic misdemeanours, so I slipped away quietly. Dad was staying at the house because Mum had gone away that afternoon – somewhere with the book club that wasn't really a book club.

'I wish I weren't going away now,' she'd said that afternoon, as she squeezed my hand.

'Me too,' I lied.

'Hey, we'll have fun. I can be a responsible adult for the evening.'

Mum didn't look convinced by Dad's promise, but he came good in the end.

Post-party, I was nearly asleep when I heard the shouts coming from the back of the house – outside somewhere.

'Get down here!' I stumbled from bed to look out the window. 'Get down here now, you fucking cheat. I want a word with you!' I tugged on my jeans and a jumper and rushed downstairs, taking each step with a thump that I worried would wake Dad. 'How did you do it, eh? How did you of all people manage it?' Her accusations came at me through the walls and, not least Dad, it occurred to me the neighbours might hear her as well. If they did then they never said anything – even after.

'You're going to wake my dad,' I spoke in a whisper when I was outside with her. Her blurry-eyed appearance was worse now, and I wondered how much more she'd had to drink before coming over.

'I left the party,' she slurred. 'They think I'm going home but I came here, to confront you.' She leaned heavy on every other word, as though this were some master plan she'd concocted. 'Did you cheat?' She staggered closer to me. 'I bet you cheated.'

'Fern, please–'

It feels naïve to say I didn't see the slap coming. But when her palm collided with my cheek the sound was deafening, and unexpected.

'What's happening?' Dad appeared then. The ringing in my ears had blocked out the sound of the back door opening. When I turned to him I was still clutching my face, as though it might fall apart if I let go. 'Kid, are you okay?'

'She's fine!' Fern was whispering then and, after all the shouting, I couldn't work out why. Unless the presence of an adult had stunned her. 'She's fine, but she's a fucking cheat.'

'Fern Norton, you watch that mouth,' Dad warned. 'What would your father say?'

She shrugged. 'I don't see him.'

'You need to get yourself home, young lady.' He was standing close to me; a protective stance, I remember thinking, and I was grateful for it. 'Go home and we'll talk about all of this in the morning when you've managed to sober yourself up.'

With every lunge and sway she made, I remember a matched gesture in my stomach as it turned over with nerves.

'Let me see,' Dad eased my hand away from my face, 'let me check.'

'I said, she's fine!' She closed the gap between us again and I remember thinking: I'm going to have to defend myself.

I had every right to defend myself.

CONFESSION

S ooner or later things catch up with you.

Dad ignored my texts for another two days. But I couldn't wait forever. I promised myself that if another phone call went unanswered I'd make a house visit; I was within my rights, I convinced myself. Typically, then, it was that call that he decided to answer. Three rings in and his shaky voice arrived on the other end of the line. I considered starting the conversation with a, 'Forgive me Father, for I have…' but he beat me to the punch.

'I'm sorry I didn't get back to you.' His voice shook midway through the sentence. 'I've been trying to work out what to say.'

'I don't know that there's a guidebook or anything.' I tried to laugh.

'No, no, I suppose not.' He went quiet but I sensed there was more. 'Will you tell her?'

'Carol?'

'Who else.'

'No.'

He sighed. 'Thank you.'

'Why would I?' I replayed the highlight reel from Fern. He'd worried then, too, that I'd blow the whistle and tell Mum. He stressed the importance of it, how she could never find out, how she'd never let it go. 'Did you ever tell Mum?'

'Christ.' He laughed. 'It never crossed my mind. She wouldn't understand, kid.' So he'd been consistent with that at least, I thought. 'Is there anything I need to worry about?'

I understood his question to mean something else; 'Is there anything I need to worry about' truthfully meant, 'Are you going to tell anyone what happened?' The answer to which was a hard no. We'd both got to this point in our lives without having to confess; it didn't feel like it would change anything to ruin the streak.

'I'm not going to talk to anyone about this, Dad–'

'Your counsellor?' he interrupted.

'No, not even him. He knows that I've remembered stuff, but he doesn't need to know what it is. He won't push me either, I don't think.' Not that I would have rushed to confess, even if Isaac did push. 'I don't think anyone needs to know.'

'But you know now.'

I snorted. 'I've always known. I just misfiled the information for a while.'

After a few seconds of quiet I noticed that his breathing had changed; it came in short sharp bursts through the speaker, punctuated by sniffs.

'Dad?'

'I'm sorry.' There was a deeper inhale then, as though he were trying to collect himself. 'I'm sorry, I just worry – I have been worried, about what you must think of me.'

'Dad, I–'

'I know that I did wrong that night, kid. Everything should have been handled better.'

'You were protecting me,' I protested. Because I really

believed he had been. 'Fern, she'd already hit me once. I honestly thought she'd hit me again, she was–'

'She was an innocent young woman.' He was crying again; his breathing was ragged, and his words frayed around the edges. 'She was an innocent young woman and I killed her!'

It was strange hearing the confession aloud, although the information wasn't new. I'd been sitting with it for days – how she'd lunged at me and how Dad and his protective instinct had moved to stop her. It was a watercolour image, still, but it was clear enough that he hadn't meant to kill her; only to stop her. He set a hand on her small shoulder and pushed her away. But Fern, drunk and hazy and unstable, hadn't held her footing. She landed hard on the ground in a puddle, with her head on the corner edge of a slab. She only bled a little.

'Kid, I'm going to need you to help me,' Dad had said. 'I'm going to need you to stop crying–'

'Dad, I'm going to need you to stop crying,' I said, and although I tried to sound gentle I wasn't convinced I had been. But he hadn't been either, at the time. 'You were protecting me and I think it's important that you remember that.'

He sniffed three times in rapid succession. 'You forgot so soon afterwards.'

'Well, apparently that's what I do.'

'How much do you have back?'

'Enough, I guess.' It was a hard question to answer; how would I know what was missing? 'I don't know whether it's everything but I don't really need everything to know what happened.' He was quiet down the phone still, and I wondered whether he needed more information – more proof. 'I remember that I helped you to move her.'

But that only made him cry more.

We'd taken her back to the woods, back to Wayfare. Dad had reasoned that the partygoers would be long gone or passed out somewhere, which would make it safe. Part of Wayfare Woodlands was already closed off by then, thanks to the beginnings of safety hazards. The council had promised several times over that they'd do something with the back end of the space, but nothing ever emerged.

'We're going to take her there, okay? That's where we're aiming for,' he'd said and through tears I agreed. 'Do you want to ruin your life over this?' he'd asked, when I'd stood at Fern's feet and sobbed further.

'Of course I don't,' I managed.

'Okay, well then you lift when I lift.'

He had the car valeted the day after. I wondered how much of Fern they'd cleaned away.

We'd taken her to a quiet spot in between a huddle of trees. I didn't ask Dad how he knew it was there. But it seemed a nice enough place; the sort of place we might have all come drinking at some point, if it hadn't been sealed off from us. We dodged and ducked the cordons and left her, surrounded by leaves and moss and mess that Dad dragged up from the nearby areas. I couldn't work out whether he'd been trying to hide her, or to make her look like she might have been comfortable. Whatever the reason, they didn't find her body for days. From the angle of her head you couldn't see the wound. And although I couldn't remember leaving – the journey from woodland to home, that is – I could remember watching Dad wash the slabs off with a bleach solution at two in the morning when we got back, before tucking me into bed – like the whole thing had been a hideous dream.

'I shouldn't have done that,' he said, finally catching his breath. 'I shouldn't have got you involved like that.'

'Dad, I was already involved.'

'But you didn't need to – Christ, you didn't need to touch her.'

'I needed to help you, though, didn't I?'

He was quiet for a few seconds before asking, 'Why is this happening?'

'The memory? Because I've been trying to find it.' I laughed. 'Well, not this memory exactly. I've been trying to find any memories, to prove that I can, to correct the reason I can't. It's not normal, Dad, you and Mum always knew that.'

'I used it to my advantage, though, and I should be ashamed of that too.'

The self-pity was starting to make me uncomfortable. 'This isn't helping, you or me.'

'I'm sorry.' More sniffing; more ragged breaths. 'Why now, though, kid?'

'Because,' I hesitated, but let the rest rush out, 'I think I've done something bad.'

EVIDENCE

A clear house means a clear mind.

I told Dad everything about Caleb – which wasn't much, considering the misplaced memories. But I leaned heavy on the gym bag and the phone, the latter of which was already sodden at the bottom of the canal. 'Why didn't you take the gym bag to the dump?' he'd asked, and I had to admit that I hadn't found it – or rather, I hadn't realised I'd found it. His fatherly advice was to try to have a clear-out in the next couple of days.

'Don't donate things,' he said, 'just scrap them.'

We made plans to see each other too. He was looking at wedding venues with Carol and he couldn't move the appointment – 'It means a lot to her,' he'd said – but I couldn't decide whether that was a good or bad reason for not acting sooner. It was best to act normal, I guessed, but still. He told me he'd pick me up outside my building at around eight in the evening; it was two days after we'd talked.

'I can come over, if you want, to save you the drive.'

'No.' He'd snapped the response. 'No, I can get you, it's fine.'

I wondered whether he wanted to keep me away from Carol.

I was into my second week off from work and I reasoned that

having been unproductive for the first few days, the least I could do was turn my flat upside down in the days that remained. My grandmother, on Mum's side, had always said a clear house was good for the mind; although I thought it would take more than rifling through my wardrobes and cupboards to unburden me. Still, I put our playlist on and let Death Cab For Cutie croon in the background while I started in the living room.

In the centre of the room there was a cardboard box that I'd planned to throw everything into. It would be easy to take to the waste dump; by easy, I meant inconspicuous. After looking through four drawers the box remained empty, and I'd started to think the living room had been the wrong plan of attack. But another three drawers in I found something; a photo frame that was mirrored around the edges, so I could catch snatches of my own face while I stared down at Caleb's. He wasn't alone in the picture; either side of him there stood a parent and although none of them were dressed formally, his Mum and Dad's expressions were ones of pride. I couldn't help but smile; it must have been a lovely moment. And I'd stolen it, I remembered; from Facebook, though, or somewhere else? I cracked the back of the frame open and took the photo out, reasoning that it would be safer to burn rather than dump, and then I threw the frame itself into the box. It landed with a heavy thud.

'Well, at least that's a start.'

I moved around the room drawer by drawer and found paraphernalia that I couldn't place owning or buying or acquiring. But it struck me as likely that everyone had those things lying around their home. I could remember Mum unpacking Christmas decorations with a frown – 'Is half of this stuff even ours?' – as she tried to place things from the year before. Time makes us forget. But still, I filled the box with anything I couldn't place because it was better to be safe than arrested.

By midday the box was half full and my dad had called three times.

'Is everything okay?' he rushed when I eventually returned the calls.

'Everything's fine, I'm just having a clear-out. I've had my music on.'

'You're okay though?'

'Yes, Dad, why?' It was a stupid question; I'd half-confessed to something that I might have done but couldn't really be sure about. Looking at it from that angle, it was more surprising that he wasn't wading through the apartment with me to hold me more accountable for the things I owned – but maybe shouldn't have owned.

'I was just...' He sighed. 'I was worried. Are we still okay for tomorrow?'

'Eight. I'll be out front.'

'Okay.' He hovered, as though wanting to say more. 'Text me, later today?'

'I'll let you know how the clear-out goes.'

'No, not for that. Will you just – Kid, let me know you're okay, okay?'

'Okay.' There was another long pause. 'I'll catch you later, Dad,' I eventually said, and I disconnected the call partway through his goodbye. He was holding me up, and I sensed there was plenty still to do.

The lyrics followed me into the bedroom and although Tegan and Sara had never been a personal favourite I still found myself singing along. I emptied the sock and underwear drawers; the towel drawers; the T-shirt drawers just above the wardrobe's crawl space. I ferreted through the memory bag again, too, to be sure the gym bag hadn't been the only thing I'd stashed. The closest I came to a discovery was a T-shirt, hung rather than folded, between my own shirts. It was soft, red and logoed to show a designer brand – and it definitely wasn't mine. I pressed the fabric against my face and took a deep inhale. And I kept it close to me while I skimmed through the remaining cupboards and hideaways.

After another two hours of searching, the T-shirt was the last thing I threw into the box. I placed it over the top of everything else – the ring of innocuous keys; the blank notebook; the three different photo frames I'd retrieved from various drawers – and then I tucked the fabric around the edges, as though safely tucking in a child. The fruits of my labours, I thought, although it might not have been an altogether appropriate way of seeing things. On top of the T-shirt I piled things I didn't mind getting rid of: a few old shirts; CDs that had become redundant; the scrapbook of teenage me that had brought only trouble. At least, if questioned, I could tell a grey lie and point to the items on top while protesting – 'Yes, of course it's all mine.' – although I didn't know who I expected to stop me and ask.

The playlist rolled around to She Wants Revenge and I sat cross-legged in front of the box. Dad had been right, of course, the clear-out was necessary. I didn't know whether all these things – this evidence – belonged to Caleb. It had crossed my mind once or twice over the afternoon they might belong to someone else entirely – thoughts that I shook away quickly, reminding myself one fire at a time was enough. All I could really be sure of was that the men's shirt that smelled like Caleb didn't belong to me. But at least I'd always have the memory.

WOODLAND

The nursery rhymes were right about surprises and the woods.

Dad collected me at eight on the dot outside my building. I'd deliberately worn dark clothes – deep-blue jeans and a black jumper – as though we were about to orchestrate a bank heist. When I climbed into the driver's seat I saw that Dad had done the same. He flashed me a tight smile and then pulled away from the kerb, waiting until we were back in traffic before he said anything.

'How are you feeling?'

'How are *you* feeling?' I leaned hard on the 'you'. Out of the two of us Dad was more likely to lose his shit, I thought.

'I'm okay, a bit nervous.'

'Wedding jitters?' He threw me a look out of the corner of his eye and a sharp laugh burst out of me. 'I'm kidding, sorry. I know it's not the time for comedy. I don't know whether it's a nervous thing or not.'

He smiled. 'I'm nervous about body-snatching with my daughter of an evening.'

'I don't know that snatching is the right word.' I looked out of the window. 'There might not even be anything to find.' When he didn't answer I shot him a look and from that alone I could read what he wasn't saying; he was sure there'd be something. 'Why did you want to drive? We could've just walked there.'

'It helps to have a car sometimes.'

'But wh–' Then it hit me. 'Oh.' I thought about how we'd bundled her in, folding her body like an origami structure until she fit through the mouth of the open trunk space. 'I understand, sorry.'

'Hey,' he caught a hold of my knee, 'let's talk about something else. How's work?'

'Pass. How's your work?'

'Better than yours by the sounds of things. We're busy at the minute. Which is good, on account of Carol having expensive taste.' He laughed. 'I thought the wedding would be more low-key than it's turning out. But whatever she wants, I guess.'

'How were the venues?'

He sighed. 'Not quite to her lady's liking.'

The pleasantries came to an abrupt halt when we pulled up at what used to be the back entrance to Wayfare Woods. Dad parked the car in a designated spot, even though the white lines were hardly visible under the years of crap and foliage that had landed on them. He put the handbrake on and took a deep breath.

'When we go in there, we need to walk straight on for about fifty yards and–'

'Dad, it's okay,' I looked towards the broken wood that passed for a gate, 'I remember how to get there.' But I couldn't place how recent the memory was.

He and I climbed out of the car without another word and made our way between the trees. Dad hadn't asked too many questions, and I wondered whether he'd been saving them for this moment.

'Why do you want to check here?' he shouted back from ahead of me.

'Because it's a safe spot.'

He turned. 'Safe how?'

'They didn't find her for days.'

We shared a horrible knowing look.

'I see.' He went back to leading, but added, 'And you can't remember anything?'

'No, Dad, nothing.' I didn't like the scepticism in his tone; he'd believed in my memory issues while they were keeping him safe, yet somehow now felt different. 'I don't just use it as an excuse, you know? Maybe when I was a kid and we'd argue, and I wouldn't want to talk about whatever had happened.' I panted as I tried to keep pace with him; my inner-city lungs playing catch-up. 'But I don't just ignore big stuff, I wouldn't just ignore–'

I collided into his back, having not realised he'd come to a stop in front of me. Dad was fixed; even my nudge hadn't broken his stare. And then I knew.

He paced a perimeter around Caleb. Dad had his fingers knotted into his hair.

'What the fuck did you do?'

'I don't know!'

It had taken him ten minutes to shake off the shock of his discovery, but anger had flooded in its place.

'How did you even – fuck! He's double your size. How did you get him here?'

'Dad, I–'

'I know, I know, you don't know.' He crouched and stared, and I saw the thoughts move through him as though they were on a rolling banner. 'What is there to tie you to him?'

With some sadness I admitted, 'Nothing.' It occurred to me then that that might have been why I'd done it; to have him, to somehow make something for the two of us. It wasn't quite the romantic ideal. But we'd always have this now.

'There's no reason for the police to come back?'

I couldn't remember telling him about the visit. But what did that count for? 'No, there's no reason. They're no more likely to visit me than they are anyone else in my building. It's been days now, they can't have found anything.'

'But the CCTV?'

'Dad, I said it's been days.'

He started to pace again. I used the time for my own crouch. Caleb must have looked like he was sleeping when I'd left him; eyes closed and mouth a little jutted open. But he looked different after over a week in the outdoors. Things had pecked and pried and nibbled, and there were wounds on him that I knew I hadn't left – although I couldn't be sure how I knew. I shook my head hard, knocking out the beginnings of a memory, and instead just watched.

'We're going to have to leave him here,' Dad eventually decided. 'There's no point moving him, because that could make things worse now. You need to go home though, kid, okay? Can you do that for me?' He raised his voice and spoke slowly, as though I were in shock – or stupid.

I nodded. 'Okay, but I could help?'

He nearly laughed. 'I can't look at you while I do this.'

The wave of shame hit me with a force. I wondered how we'd managed this the last time – why he was willing to manage it now. He didn't owe me anything; nothing more than the average parent owes the average child anyway. But I knew this went above and beyond average. I decided it must be guilt over something. Fern? Maybe. Even though she'd been an accident, I could see the mirrored then and now and he must have spotted it too. Although he hadn't watched her; he hadn't waited. He hadn't meant to–

'Come on now.' He spoke gently to catch my attention. 'I need you to stick with me.'

'Why are you doing this?'

He rolled up his sleeves. 'What do you mean?'

'Helping me. Helping me to hide this. Why would you do that?'

He sighed, rubbed his temples and looked at Caleb while he answered. 'Because I'm your father, and this is what parents do for their kids. They clean up after them.' He huffed and smiled; it looked like the prelude to a laugh. 'Granted, I thought this stopped at washing drunken up-chucks off the garden patio. But sure, this makes sense as well.'

This makes sense... I parroted back.

'Dad, I...' I petered out when I saw his hand raise.

'I think less is more is probably a good measure, kiddo. I'm helping, can we leave it?'

I nodded, then pulled a big breath in. 'I don't want this to ruin my life, Dad,' I said, borrowing his words to a younger version of myself. He'd done something very different and I knew that, but the sentiment still carried. I paid close attention to my tone and tried to make the admission crack somewhere in the middle. 'I don't,' I started to shake my head, 'I just don't want this to ruin my life.'

He closed the distance between us and set a hand either side of my face, to keep my gaze. It was something he'd done when I was younger; something he'd copied from Mum, I remembered, when he thought I wasn't listening to him.

'Hey, I'm going to need you to stop crying, kid, okay?' I hadn't even realised that I'd started. 'I don't want this to ruin your life either. So I'm going to fix this, okay? I just need to make sure there isn't anything here that shouldn't be here. I've got a torch in the back of the car, and I'll grab a bag too, just in case, and then I'll fix this.'

I nodded along with every part of the suggestion, then asked, 'Can I stay?'

He narrowed his eyes, and I imagined him trying to weigh up where I'd be more of a liability; here or away. 'Sure, sure you can wait.' He let go of me then. 'You stay here and I'll be right back with the stuff. You're okay here though? You're okay to watch him?'

I flashed a tight smile in agreement. I'd managed six months; another few minutes would be fine.

CAROL

When someone scratches your back there's a time when they'll need the same courtesy.

Dad had let me stay with him while he scouted the area for anything that might belong to me. But in among the discarded condoms, empty beer bottles and party poppers from yesteryear, there wasn't anything I could claim ownership of. It seemed an unholy grave to leave a man in, but I'd made it this far without anyone finding anything to lead them here. Dad wrapped a carrier bag around each hand and sucked in a deep pull of air before he lifted Caleb softly, rolling him onto one side and then the other. I flashed the beam of light under him, looking for personal possessions buried in the sodden ground.

'There's nothing, Dad.'

Each time he'd lowered him back with care and I was grateful for it.

'Okay, we're good to go.'

It was the early hours of the following morning when he dropped me off outside my building again. I invited him in for tea – 'You can even stay here for the night, if you want to?' – but he declined my politeness.

'I need to get back to Carol.'

I checked my watch to be sure. 'It's nearly three in the morning.'

'Still, I'd rather get home.'

There was a tension between us. 'Okay. Okay sure, that makes sense.' I climbed out of the car, somewhat reluctantly, and when I'd keyed in the code for the building I looked back to wave him off. He'd already left, though, without the evening-time traffic to slow him down.

I'd slept fitfully in the hours that followed. First on the sofa, listening to the Dave Matthews Band but when the playlist was exhausted I made a move for the bed. I thought of texting Dad to check in – *Will he even be at work?* – but reasoned that he might also be taking the morning to sleep restlessly in one room then another.

It was nearly midday when I woke up for the final time. There was a thunderous banging against the front door and I thought, *This must be it then; they must be coming to get me.* But on the stretch of the hallway I managed to talk myself out of the idea. I didn't look through the spyhole but slammed the locks straight open and pulled at the door.

'Carol?'

'I'm so sorry just to drop in.'

She didn't look sorry, but I wasn't going to fight her on it. 'No, no it's fine. What are families for?' I laughed. 'Is everything okay – did something...' I trailed off, hoping she might fill in the blank. I caught a shift in one of her legs, and she looked past me along the hallway. 'Did you want to come in?'

'Oh, if I could?'

'Sure,' I pulled the door back, 'come right in.' *This is just what was missing from the last eighteen hours,* I thought as I padded along behind her. 'Straight ahead is the kitchen, if you want to head in. You can talk to me while I make us some tea.'

'Milk, one sugar,' she said, already leaning back against the counter.

I set the kettle boiling. 'Is everything okay?' I tried again.

'Look, I – I don't mean.' She stopped, sighed, restarted. 'Have you ever been married?'

I laughed. 'I like to think I've evolved beyond that.'

'Of course.' She at least managed a chuckle then. 'You kids. But, when you're about to marry someone, you get all these worries, do you know what I mean?' I didn't but I nodded all the same, then turned to get mugs from the cupboard. 'You get all these worries and you start to wonder whether you're doing the right thing and whether you really want–'

'I'm sorry,' I interrupted, 'are you trying to tell me you don't want to marry Dad?'

'Hell, not even. I'm trying – well, I suppose – what I'm trying to say is...'

'That he doesn't want to marry you.'

'Did he tell you that?' she snapped, then settled again. 'I'm sorry – you weren't – I mean, he hasn't. Has he?'

I flashed her a thin smile. 'Did something happen?'

'I'm being an old fool, I think, most likely.' I crossed to grab the milk from the fridge while she yammered. 'If I ask you something, will you be honest?'

That depends on the question. I was glad to be facing away from her. 'Of course.'

She took a deep pull of air. 'Was he with you last night?'

The milk overspilled from the carton and splashed onto the work surface. 'Shit.' I reached for a cloth and turned to face her while I spoke. 'That's what you want to ask?'

'He said he was. But he came home so late and – do you think I'm dreadful?'

'Not remotely.' I handed her a mug. 'But he was with me last night. Until around three, I guess? I was having a moment. Mum didn't answer so I called him. Around eight, maybe? I'm not so good with times, exactly. But he was with me.'

She sighed and smiled. 'You must think I'm an old fool.'

'A woman in love, I think.' I took a sip of hot tea. 'Although they're very similar.'

She crossed the kitchen then and set her drink down on the counter behind me. She pressed her palms against my upper arms and rubbed, as though trying to build friction – but I knew the more likely intention was to convey sympathy. 'I'm chattering on about nothing at all and here you are. Are you okay? Did your Dad help?'

It felt quite different, being able to give these honest answers. *Truthful people must feel like this all the time.* I smiled at her. 'He really did, yeah. He was great.'

'You know you can call me, too, right? I don't know it all but...'

'Thanks, Carol, that's really kind.' I sensed the moment called for something, so I leaned in and gave her a tight hug. 'You too, any time. Even if it's about Dad.'

I wouldn't be a snitch for her but I thought it might comfort her to think otherwise. I'd lost track of who was giving who alibis now. But wherever the grey lies were, Dad and I were in it together.

HOMEWORK

Sometimes you have to plan and work and plan to get at things.

After two days Dad stopped asking whether I'd remembered anything. He'd stressed the importance of trying – 'You need to work out what happened, kid, whether there's anything we need to be worrying about here.' – but applying pressure never did get me to do anything; although it had always been the first tactic he'd tried. I told him twenty times over there was nothing to worry about – 'You can't possibly know that,' he'd replied – but somehow I did.

There were three days left of my holiday – or compassionate leave, whatever it was being called at the office – and I resolved to use them well. The first time I tried to pull a memory together I got snapshots that didn't belong in a sequence. There were men and women I didn't recognise; 'Do I know you?' asked on repeat but by different voices; once, there was even a memory of Fern. She and I had been talking amicably in that one; exchanging techniques for tying our hair up, which felt like a jarringly innocent conversation to recall. But again, I didn't know what of it belonged to Caleb. Isaac had told me it could be the right topic but the wrong talk, when I'd first started to remember snippets of Fern's death, but I couldn't stretch my belief to fit the idea of Caleb and I swapping hair tips.

I left the curtains open; there was nothing to distract me anymore. Then I set the Newton's cradle to tick in the background. I practised breathing – in through the belly up through the lungs and back again – and tried to focus on Caleb. After 103 clinks of ball on ball – in through the belly – I remembered something; a mirrored image of me. Up through the lungs – I remembered tying my hair into a tight and high ponytail – and back again – and then placing a cap over the top of my head. The memory was recent – in through the belly – it wasn't from me and Fern but now – up through the lungs – and once I'd adjusted the cap three or four times, the mirror image went away, rippled out like a dream sequence – and back again. I was wearing dark clothes and I could remember pulling on black gloves – in through the belly – but I wasn't sure whether it was for warmth or practicality.

Like a slipped film reel – up through the lungs – I was outside a building and the intercom was broken which meant the gate was hanging wide – and back again – so I walked right in. There were seven flights to climb, so it must have been his building; he was on a level floor to my own. In through the belly – I drew in a deep breath and pounded up the stairs, taking one floor at a time but pausing after four sets – up through the lungs – but I remember wanting to be out of breath, panting even when I banged on the door.

'Do I know you?'

He was so beautiful.

'I'm so – sorry – I'm a friend – of Louise's.' I paused and made a show of sucking in air – and back again, in through the belly – before I carried on. 'We were having a night – a campfire catch-up.' I nearly laughed – up through the lungs – but I didn't have the air for it. 'She fell – the others, they're waiting – there's an ambulance – not there yet but coming.'

'Jesus, is she okay?'

And back again – I remember thinking what a stupid question it was. I shook my head.

'We think it's her leg – it might be broken – we're not – we're not totally sure. She asked,' I paused to gulp air again – in through the belly up through the lungs. 'She asked one of us to come and get you.'

'Why didn't she call?' he asked as he shrugged on a jacket. His T-shirt rode up to show the curve of his stomach – and back again, in through the belly – and I saw a sliver of brown hair make an arrow to his crotch. I could have kissed it – up through the lungs – how I'd seen her do it.

'She did, but your phone wasn't ringing out.'

He looked behind him – and back again – and then rushed for his phone, balanced on the arm of the sofa. 'There aren't any calls. Fuck it, what does it matter?' He stashed the handset in his pocket – in through the belly – and grabbed his keys from the sideboard. 'Did you drive, run, what?' He pulled the door closed behind him.

'Walked, ran a little.' I laughed and he reciprocated.

'I get it, I'm not all that fit either.'

Oh, but he was.

'There's a shortcut,' I said, heading back for the stairs – up through the lungs and back again – but I turned to face him. 'The lift took forever when I called it.'

'Always does,' he nodded to the steps behind me, 'your lead.'

In through the belly – I paced back down the stairs and heard Caleb's mirror-steps behind me – up through the lungs – and I held my breath as best as I could until we were outside the building – and back again – but I couldn't remember whether it was excitement or nerves or – in through the belly. He took an immediate left turn when we were outside, and I caught his arm and choked on my breath at the contact.

'Are you okay?' He set a hand on my back.

'Sorry, winded.' Up through the lungs. 'There's a shortcut. The main road takes forever.' And back again – the main road had CCTV; the lift would have had–

He followed me dutifully – in through the belly – and made idle conversation while we walked. I didn't even have to prompt him – up through the lungs – to tell me how little he really knew of Louise – and back again, in through the belly – and how they'd only been seeing each other for a while; I knew it was a lie but I didn't mind. His voice sounded different to how I'd expected it to but somehow suited him perfectly all the same. Up through the lungs – he asked me about myself and I was honest – and back again – because it didn't matter what he knew. Who was he going to tell?

'Wayfare Woods? This is where you were having a campfire?'

In through the belly – I nodded and trod ahead. 'It's dead quiet around here.'

'I can't see an ambulance or anything,' he said – up through the lungs – and I thought he sounded suspicious of something but he still followed me – and back again. 'You're sure this is the spot where you left them all?'

I stumbled. I remember the feeling of hard earth against my knee – in through the belly – and Caleb dropping next to me to check I was okay – up through the lungs and back again – and I was fine because I'd engineered the fall; this pause, this closeness. In through the belly –

'You're shaking,' he said, touching my back again. He trod around me to get a front view – up through the lungs and back again – and he lifted my hand away from my knee, where I was clutching at the faux injury – in through the belly – in through the belly – in through – his touch was the most gentle thing. 'Are you okay?'

'Cold, adrenaline too, you know?'

He smiled at me, in a pitiful sort of way but I didn't mind – up through the lungs. He loosened his jacket from around his shoulders and draped it around mine.

'You need this more than I do.' He stayed crouched with me. 'Are you ready?'

In through the belly up through the lungs and back. I nodded. 'I think so.'

He held out a hand for me to grab, which I did – in through the belly – and he tugged me into a standing position – up through the lungs and back again – and then he turned to face the quiet trees and – in through the belly – I followed him and–

The memory wouldn't come, and I wouldn't force it.

After that, I decided, anything could have happened.

FAMILY

Bonding comes in different forms.

Mum asked if we could all have dinner together; all three of us, for the first time in what I guessed would be around ten years. The invite came via text message which at least gave me time to consider viable excuses. But in the end I agreed and asked whether she could make it this weekend. She replied only minutes later to say they could both do Saturday evening. The speed of her response made me wonder whether they'd already discussed possible times and dates; or whether they were together. I didn't ask. Instead I replied to ask her what I could bring and she, in a mumsy fashion, said, 'Your appetite'.

When I arrived at Mum's front door, Dad opened it.

'Family bonding time?' I asked and raised an eyebrow. He pulled me into a tight hug without replying, and a full twenty seconds passed with him just holding me. When he let go he held me by the shoulders and looked me up and down as though inspecting me. 'Dad, what–'

'I'll always be here for you, do you know that?' he said in a low whisper, to avoid Mum catching the assurance, I guessed.

'Yeah, of course. Seriously, what–'

'I mean it, kid, always.' He leaned hard on the last word. 'What do you remember?'

'Dad, come on, I already told you.'

'From the last week, kid. What do you remember from the last week?'

It filtered in like a montage: Fern and finding Caleb and dumping the evidence and watching his body. 'Everything.'

He gave my shoulders a squeeze. 'That's good. It's really good that you haven't lost it.' I flashed a sincere smile, because he was probably right. The high stress levels of the last week would have normally caused black holes everywhere. But somehow this was all different. 'Your mother has made enough to feed an army, so get in.'

Down the hallway and in the kitchen, Mum, juggling a saucepan of potatoes, leaned across at an angle to kiss my cheek.

'Anything I can do?' I asked, with my head already in the fridge to scout for a pre-dinner snack.

'Your dad is helping,' she said and when my head snapped around I saw the raised eyebrow, and the smirk. 'He's trying to help.'

Half an hour later we all huddled around Mum's dining-room table with a meal that looked fit to feed a family double our size. I wondered how much of it Dad was responsible for; setting the table, I suspected, or maybe bringing the ice cream for pudding. Everyone coasted through the meal with appreciative murmurs and cutlery clicking against crockery. Mum's plate was near empty when she set her knife and fork down – one implement either side, still, so I knew she hadn't finished eating – and cleared her throat.

'Your dad and I want to talk to you, about what's happening between us.'

'Shots fired,' I said and smiled, with mashed potato filling my cheeks. I swallowed hard and said, 'I wondered when that would come up.'

Dad reached across the table to squeeze Mum's hand and I couldn't make the image fit my map of them.

'We're not going to see each other anymore,' he announced, saving Mum a job.

'We've decided it's not fair,' she added. 'There's you to consider, and of course, there's Carol. So, your Dad and I will put a stop to it, effective immediately,' she pulled her hand away as though making a stand, 'but, if we can ask a favour, we'd like for Carol not to know.'

I looked from one of them to the other. 'You want me to lie to her?'

'A grey lie,' Mum said.

'When would it even come up?' I asked.

'At the hen party, over tea, during the wedding. Christ.' Dad sounded flustered. He'd dealt with a dead body easier than infidelity which I thought explained a lot about him – and maybe me. 'I just don't want life to be turned upside down because your Mum and I had a moment.' He shook his head. 'A few moments.'

'Love, it helps all of us to keep this to ourselves.'

I chewed slowly and tried to draft a response. 'I think it helps you two more than me.'

'Kid, we've all got secrets, right?' Dad held direct eye contact with me; the stare was unsettling, and I knew what he was trying to say with it. So much for always protecting me, I thought. 'Everyone has things they'd rather other people didn't know about. This is ours.'

'Okay.' I set my knife and fork down. 'Is there afters or do I need to pop out?'

They shared a look. 'That's it?' Mum asked.

'Dad's right, isn't he? Everyone has something.' I leaned over and punched his arm gently; a trace of childhood that was left from my weekends with him. 'Don't look so worried.'

He laughed. 'Well, okay then.'

Mum collected her cutlery and tucked into the remaining dregs of food. 'Your dad brought ice cream for afters, but he needs to deal with the washing-up first.' She winked; he rolled his eyes. It was like we were a normal family.

When Mum had finished she encouraged Dad into the kitchen to tackle the mountain of washing-up. 'I can help with that,' I offered but it was met with resistance from them both.

'Your dad will be fine.' She grabbed my elbow to steer me out of the kitchen. 'We'll throw the television on for some background noise and have a chat. Dad'll bring the ice cream in when he's finished. Won't you, love?' She didn't wait for an answer.

The familiarity of it all did something to warm my insides. 'This has been nice,' I said, wedging myself against the arm of the sofa. 'All of us being together like this.'

'Just like old times?'

'Not really. You two like each other a lot more now.'

She laughed but then caught my expression. 'Oh, love, I'm so sorry that you–'

'Really,' I held up a hand, 'we don't need to bring that stuff up.'

Mum didn't say anything else, she just flicked the television on and waited for the click of the screen warming up. She thumbed to the evening news, which seemed an odd choice for background chatter, but I let her have it.

'It makes me feel better about my own life,' she said with a half-chuckle and I wondered whether she'd caught something in my expression. 'Plus, good to know what's happening. Where's that ice cream?' she shouted.

'On its way, woman, on its way.'

'How are you feeling about going back to work?' she asked.

'Okay, mostly, I think. It will be good to keep occupied again.'

'Do you think the break helped?'

I thought over the montage. 'It helped me to get some things sorted.'

'This just in…'

I tried not to look at the news report while Mum talked. 'Well that's good, at least.'

'How's everything with you right now? Anyone on the scene?' *Apart from Dad*, I thought, but didn't say.

'Police are reporting a discovery…'

'I've been off the online dating because of,' she nodded toward the kitchen, 'but I think it'll be good for me to get back on the horse. How about you? You were seeing someone?'

'Although nothing has been confirmed from a spokesperson yet…'

'I brought a bowl of chocolate and a bowl of strawberry and there's vanilla waiting in the kitchen. How about we just dig in?' Dad announced.

'Chocolate first though, right?' I heard Mum say but I couldn't look away from the television. There were muted blue lights being filmed from a distance and patrol cars sealing off the entrance. 'Love?' Someone appeared in a white coverall suit and gloves and–

'The body is believed to be male with early speculation guessing…'

'Kid, you with us?'

'…that it might be missing businessman, Caleb Neale.'

PART VI

TIME

I am not an honest person at heart.

Thirteen months have rolled by since they found him. There has been canvassing, there have been witness appeals; further door-to-door enquiries and even one arrest that turned out to be a false alarm. For a flicker I thought I might say something then, to stop an innocent man going to prison for a guilty woman; only for a flicker though. The appeals happen less frequently now, and from social media sleuthing I found out recently that Tuesday is seeing someone new. She's still involved with the police campaigns although they're few and far between. And I'm glad to know she isn't pining. The Redhead seems to be, from her depressing daily posts on grief; but Caleb was never really hers to lose, only mine to take.

I've moved too. There was too much residual energy in my old building, so I waited what felt like an unsuspicious amount of time before calling in estate agents. Throughout the viewings there were all manner of weird and wonderful couples seen into the place. Plus one solo viewer who came in and stared through my living-room window for five minutes before saying he didn't know whether the flat was the right fit.

'It's a killer view,' I said, half-joking. But he still didn't bite.

In the end a young couple took the place off my hands. They didn't have a property chain either, so it was a swift changeover for me. I packed boxes with the help from Dad but not Mum, because I could trust him more than her these days. Then one happy weekend we loaded everything into a van and moved me to a little house just outside the city, on a freshly built plot with a neat street that had barely been broken in by tyres.

I haven't unpacked yet. There's one box – full of things that could belong to anyone – that Dad put straight into my small attic. He marked the cardboard lid as '*Miscellaneous*' and winked at me as he loaded it into the truck. There are other boxes all over the place, though, and it's likely they'll stay there for a while. I've been trying to get to know the neighbourhood, and the neighbours, and getting used to the commute to work. But there are perks to living outside of city limits, even if the walk to the office has become a drive.

In the bathroom mirror – one that's big and bright and not yet stained with watermarks – I follow the line of my lips with a soft pink lipstick, and then pucker and pop them to see that there aren't any stray lines. I was in comfortable clothing still, but that was no excuse not to make an effort with the parts that people might see; the kitchen window was waist high and anyone could look in while I was washing, cutting and chopping. I always wear lipstick now.

On the way down the stairs I have to shimmy between boxes of books that need to be unpacked and alphabetised in the room that Mum calls my 'Home office'. Although I don't know what she thinks I'm likely to do in there. In synchronicity with me landing on the ground floor my phone's shrill ringtone kicks in from somewhere in the kitchen. It's vibrating along the kitchen table and I catch it just before it drops from the edge.

'Hi, Dad.'

'Hey, kid. Just checking in.' He does this more now. 'Good day?'

'Long. How about yours?'

'Boring.' He laughs. 'Are you busy tonight?'

I look at the roasting dinner of vegetables waiting for the oven. 'Not really. Why?'

'Can you tell Carol you are?'

'Why?' I lean back on the table, waiting for the grey lie.

'She said we should just stop in to see you, which I said was rude without calling. So, she said I should call and here we are.'

'You don't want to come over?'

He lowers his voice. 'I have plans.'

'But you don't need an alibi?'

He laughs. 'Would I ask?' *Yes*, I think. 'No, I don't need one, thanks.'

'Dad...' I think about asking. But I can't decide whether I really want to know. 'Be careful, whatever you're doing?'

'You too, kid. You call me if you need me?'

'Sure thing, always.'

We say our goodbyes and disconnect. I try to meddle less, but I know he'll call if he needs me and after last year I suspect he feels the same. I roll up the sleeves of my soft jumper and thumb through the cutlery drawer, pulling out utensils and plate settings. She'll be home soon and I want dinner to be ready. It might seem strange, given history, but these days I feel closer to her than ever – and it's just nice to feel close to someone.

When the table is set, I slide the baking tray into the oven and set the timer. I thumb through our playlist and allow myself the luxury of a dance around the kitchen to Duran Duran, which is the best workout I can muster these days. When I'm halfway through the song I go back to base, though, and bury my hands in the warm water of the washing-up bowl; I like to get everything clean and cleared away.

There's a hum of an engine from up the road somewhere. Not for the first time, I think what a benefit it is to hear those early signs of arrival.

I sing along to the music still, but pause to pucker my lips as I hear the car engine cut out. By the time I've dried my hands and gone back to the sink – the window – she's there. Across the road I watch her walk into the matching kitchen layout and kiss the man on the cheek – I haven't christened him anything yet, it's too soon. She stands behind him and wraps her arms around his waist, and when she peers round to look at him her face is just visible. The last year hasn't changed her much; although she doesn't have sex in front of the window with this one. I keep my hands in the bowl, looking down at regular intervals to maintain the illusion. Across the road, Tuesday tells the man about her day at work. And I watch.

THE END

A NOTE FROM THE PUBLISHER

Thank you for reading this book. If you enjoyed it please do consider leaving a review on Amazon to help others find it too.

We hate typos. All of our books have been rigorously edited and proofread, but sometimes mistakes do slip through. If you have spotted a typo, please do let us know and we can get it amended within hours.

info@bloodhoundbooks.com